RUNNING SCARED

The Second PETE CULNANE MYSTERY

S.L. SMITH

BEAVER'S
POND
PRESS

ISBN 13: 978-1-59298-970-6

Library of Congress Catalog Number: 2013914153

Printed in the United States of America

First Printing: 2013

17 16 15 14 13   5 4 3 2 1

Beaver's Pond Press, Inc.
7108 Ohms Lane
Edina, MN 55439–2129
(952) 829-8818
www.BeaversPondPress.com

To order, visit www.BeaversPondBooks.com
or call (800) 901-3480. Reseller discounts available.

To my grandmother, Agnes (Gregory) Heinen,
a centenarian with a quick wit and marvelous sense of humor who,
throughout her life, lived independently, dressed to the nines,
stood ramrod straight, and had a spring in her step.

PROLOGUE

For the eighth straight day, fear dictated Nick's thoughts and actions.

Until recently, Nick Rice clung religiously to a schedule that included rolling out of bed at seven in the morning and shutting down his brain as he slid between the sheets at midnight. He believed it maximized his productivity. He was right. That no longer mattered. The days when these preferences were a consideration now felt like "the good old days."

Nick had reluctantly adopted a new routine. It meant beginning his daily run in the middle of the night. Granted, five thirty in the morning isn't the middle of the night for everyone. Even so, that's how it felt to him. The fact that during the winter it was still pitch black in Minnesota at that hour supported Nick's contention.

All of this began with a sporadic feeling of being watched. As the days passed, these feelings increased. Intuitive by nature, Nick trusted his instincts. If anything, he was a realist. As a result, his irritation with this intrusion evolved into anger. Next came frustration over his inability to identify or even get a glimpse of his stalker. Anxiety followed.

Now he lived in fear.

Nick began questioning his sanity. He considered seeing a psychiatrist. Then reality reared its ugly head. The only way to keep those appointments out of his medical records was to eat the cost. Despite the mandates, Nick knew healthcare records weren't adequately protected. Refusing to risk the possible repercussions on his career, he abandoned that consideration. Besides, he wasn't crazy.

Constant and ongoing efforts to get a glimpse of his pursuer were the only challenge to that belief. An outsider might interpret this as an obsessive-compulsive disorder. This predicament didn't affect his work performance or his productivity—despite inadequate sleep and the disruptions to his normal schedule. Even so, the longer this continued, the more desperate he became. He found a measure of reassurance in knowing that no one in his family was ever diagnosed with a mental illness.

He told friends his sister was experiencing this problem and asked for their advice. He knew that had all the markings of going to the doctor and asking about a friend's symptoms. Even so, he was unable to devise a better plan. He hoped his friends would buy his story. When one friend began pressing for the truth, Nick abandoned that ploy.

He considered discussing this with his wife. Heather knew something was bothering him. She broached the subject, but he insisted she'd imagined it. Wishful thinking? Perhaps, but she wouldn't understand. Women tend to be more intuitive than men, or so he'd heard. Heather was an exception. She denied the existence of intuition as a reliable phenomenon.

He thought about the Myers-Briggs personality inventory. His last boss thought it would solve the company's personnel issues. Wrong, but Nick found the tool both interesting and useful. The test ranked him as a strong "N," suggesting he intuitively assessed and interpreted what he saw and heard.

Out of curiosity and to validate his perceptions, he asked Heather to take the test. She ranked as a strong "S." Spot on. Generally, she accepted things at face value.

Nick had another reason not to discuss this problem with Heather. She tended to be an alarmist. If he gave her any indication that he, she, or their three kids were in danger, she wouldn't drop it. She'd go into overdrive, looking for a solution. She wouldn't let up before she had a plan, implemented it, and solved the problem. She'd talk about it ad nauseam. Then two things would be driving Nick over the edge.

Nick's conscience grabbed him by the throat and dragged him back to reality. He wasn't being fair. Heather was a blessing. Their marriage had its problems, but he loved her and was committed to making it work. She brought out the best in him. She helped him in countless, unacknowledged ways.

Thanks to her, their family survived the year he was unemployed. He'd spent an average of sixty hours a week searching for a job on the Internet, networking, and knocking on doors. After some radical adjustments to their lifestyle, the money she made as a management consultant paid the bills and kept the family solvent.

She kept more than their finances afloat. She kept his ego from crashing and burning as he was passed over time and time again. She created ways to demonstrate his value to her and the kids. At one low point, she had the kids competing to see who could devise the longest list of reasons he was the world's best dad. No wonder he was crazy about her.

She'd talked him through his nervousness over accepting a job he feared might compromise his earning potential for years. She was right. Taking that job positioned him for the promotion that came within a year at Regisson Medical, an up-and-coming medical device company. Now, as a VP, he managed tech support.

Although it drove him to distraction at times, Nick admired Heather's ability to work nonstop on a project. She reveled in the completion. He was on the opposite end of the spectrum. He enjoyed the process and contended there was often as much to be gained from the effort as the completion. Their two perspectives kept things in balance. Family projects were accomplished, and the time frame didn't push any of them off a cliff.

Halfway through his daily run, Nick's thoughts returned to his nemesis. Until his displeasure with the problem transitioned into fear, he'd concentrated almost as much on coping with the situation as reversing it. That's why he changed his schedule. He also traded his fixed running route for a random selection from four options.

This way, he hoped to be in a location other than the one under surveillance.

Nick resumed his search for a solution. With a psychiatrist not an answer, and his friends of little help, he sought to expand the possibilities.

He grew accustomed to checking incessantly to catch the person back there. He did it on the sly—so rapidly that he hoped his pursuer couldn't anticipate the moves. Repeatedly, this effort failed.

He drove different routes to work. His work schedule was flexible, so he added more variety, leaving home and returning at atypical hours.

He stopped eating lunch at the usual places and times. Heather was amazed when he announced that he'd pack his lunch several days each week. He told her that working through lunch meant he got home earlier; and she either bought it, or let it pass and assumed she'd eventually learn the truth.

He even changed the church he and his family attended. To justify it, he researched several churches and their special programs. He concocted a story about switching to one that encouraged its congregation to go green. Heather asked about his unanticipated but welcome "conversion." He hugged her and said she didn't give herself enough credit for her influence on him and their kids.

Nick hated all this lying. He loved variety, but hated changes forced upon him. He liked to be in charge of his life. He despised having an unidentified threat ruling this thoughts and actions.

It seemed imperative that he eliminate the problem. But how?

He couldn't run away. Even if he quit his job, Heather couldn't do that. The network she depended upon centered on the Twin Cities. Uprooting the family in the middle of the school year and moving without notice would be hard on all of the kids—especially Alexis. The introvert of the family, she found it difficult to make friends and deal with even small changes. Fleeing in the middle of the night would qualify as total upheaval, especially during his daughter's first year of middle school. The transition from grade school to middle school, and all the changes that entailed, had been traumatic. Nick couldn't put his daughter through that much turmoil a second time in one school year.

His boys were more resilient. Tyler, his second child, qualified as the extreme extrovert in the family. Without giving it a second thought, Tyler would walk up to a group of kids, introduce himself, and fit in instantly.

Danny fell somewhere between Alexis and Tyler. He hung close to his big brother and depended upon Tyler to orchestrate his nonschool hours. Close in age, this worked for both boys. Nick hoped that Danny would acquire self-assurance by osmosis, if through no other means.

Thoughts about his kids prompted Nick to again look for any activity around him—both nearby and as far as he could see. As he turned to check behind him, his eyes scanned rooftops and windows, pausing for a moment on each parked car. He knew the stalker was out there. He felt it in his bones. But where?

When it became apparent that living under surveillance would persist, he'd spent a lot of time looking for an explanation. He hadn't slept with anyone's wife or girlfriend. Nor had he slept with anyone's husband or boyfriend. He had no links to the mortgage debacle. He hadn't stolen anyone's job or edged anyone out of a promotion. He hadn't witnessed anything unlawful or gotten a loan from an unscrupulous source.

Why else did people develop grudges, start deadly feuds, or kill one another? Didn't love and money qualify as the most common reasons? How could that apply to him?

Try as he might, Nick Rice couldn't think of anyone who would want to kill him, or even harm him. Sure, he had a few enemies. He hadn't always taken a popular approach to problem solving at work, but he didn't think the sentiments could be extreme enough to merit the time and energy this surveillance effort required.

Was murder the goal? Kidnapping? He and Heather didn't have enough money to make that profitable. Would his watcher be happy with scaring him? Was this simply a matter of sport? Not likely!

Intuition told him an attack loomed. It didn't explain why it was taking so long to implement. When and where would it happen?

His thoughts turned to the form the attack might take. Would he be shot? That seemed more likely, but less optimistic than being assaulted with a knife. In the case of a knife, he might successfully fight off his attacker. Would his food be poisoned? Unlikely. Even so, he'd taken steps to reduce that danger. What were the other possibilities?

Poison darts? Yeah, right. A bomb in his car? Possibly. He thought about ways to protect himself from one. It would be difficult, if not impossible. There were so many opportunities to get at his car. He'd need a bodyguard to protect himself from all of them.

A bodyguard. He hadn't thought of that. Finding and affording one could be a problem, but it was a viable solution. Better yet, he would hire a private investigator.

What a brilliant idea! Any PI worth his or her salt could identify the person tailing him. Then, equipped with that information, he'd attack and eliminate the problem. He could get a restraining order. No, from all he'd heard, they weren't worth the effort. The PI would help him find a solution.

How would he find the best PI? One of Heather's cousins was a cop. He could ask her. No, that would raise all sorts of questions. Worse yet, all sorts of suspicions.

Did LinkedIn have a page for PIs? It must. He'd check as soon as he got home. Roughly one mile and closing.

Near the end of his run, Nick felt physically drained, but relaxed. His emotions edged toward a more balanced state. He felt optimistic. He felt the tension flow from his back and shoulders. He felt great!

This reprieve was short-lived.

ONE

Pete Culnane was a creature of habit. For him, a daily run was a fact of life. At six o'clock this crisp winter morning, he ran along Wheelock Parkway. There was little room to negotiate the timing of his daily run. The location, on the other hand, was dictated by the time of year and snow cover.

When running in the winter, he appreciated unseasonably warm temperatures. This year, that was the case more often than not. A few days ago, he heard that meteorologists attributed the warmth and lack of snow to La Niña with a North Atlantic oscillation. Whatever the reason, this morning's temperature was in the high twenties. That was warmer than the average high for this time of year. The only snow on the ground was the remnants of the few inches that fell the first few days of January.

Last year, both St. Paul and Minneapolis burned through their October through April snow removal budgets before the end of December. This winter, to date, neither had declared a single snow emergency.

The runner in Pete relished the snow-free conditions. The skier in him longed for a foot or two of fresh powder.

Contemplating the benefits of the lack of snow reminded Pete of his aunt. Childhood onset diabetes left her legally blind. When walking on snowy sidewalks, she couldn't tell where the sidewalks ended and the snowbanks began. She laughed about it, but he knew it had to be exasperating. Witnessing her limitations gave him a deeper appreciation for the benefits of 20/20 vision.

Pete only skied about a dozen times each winter. Although he loved last winter's ski conditions, he knew he had no right to complain. And the unseasonable warmth meant he didn't have to bundle up for his run. This morning, his garb included sweatpants, a long-sleeved T-shirt, a hooded sweatshirt, and gloves. On days even a bit colder than this, he rarely wore a stocking cap. His thick and wavy dark brown hair inhibited a loss of body heat through the top of his head almost as well as a cap would.

This felt like a crazy way to dress for an early morning run this time of year. But this January was unusual, and he made the most of it.

Although Pete liked running around Lake Phalen during the months when there was daylight at this hour, he stuck with better-lit routes when he ran predawn. This month, he took advantage of the lack of snow and the grassy median strip down the center of Wheelock Parkway to preserve his knees. The gently rolling terrain added to the workout, and Pete appreciated the variety.

Each morning, he drove from home to a city street that angled off Wheelock Parkway a short distance east of Arcade. As he began running, the aromas of Italian sauce and freshly baked bread wafting from Romolo's Pizza made him hungry.

He ran down the center of the median. Before long, the scenery and his thoughts made him forget his stomach.

Along Pete's four-mile roundtrip, he passed through a portion of St. Paul's East Side. An eclectic neighborhood bordered Wheelock Parkway, and the architecture transitioned as the distance from Arcade increased. It included traditional, Tudor, Spanish, Georgian, and farmhouse styles. Two-story homes dominated. Moving towards I-35E, the size and value of the houses tended to diminish.

Oak and cedar lined the median, leaving a path down the center for Pete. Groupings of forty-foot white pine and blue spruce intermittently violated that corridor. Their branches began inches above the ground, creating a slalom course.

At this hour, lights were on in only a few homes. Walkers, other runners, and moving cars were rare. Much of the neighborhood still slept.

Pete thought about the day ahead. He wanted to wrap up the plethora of paperwork from a murder investigation that just closed. It was a gruesome case. Reports often ran hundreds of pages and were by far his least favorite part of the job. He'd recommended a few ways to expedite the process, but his suggestions were welcomed only marginally better than the St. Paul Cathedral welcomed pigeons. He smiled and shook his head. The pigeons' love for the Cathedral was unrequited.

Pete's thoughts shifted to Katie Benton. He began dating her five months ago. He really liked her, but he struggled with feelings of disloyalty to his deceased wife, Andrea. Sure, that was crazy. Andrea would tell him that, if she could. His conscious mind knew it, too. It didn't matter. The problem was with his subconscious. More specifically, his dreams were the problem.

Each time he and Katie went out, he woke up in the middle of the night, dreaming Andrea was there with him. Then he sank into a deep blue funk for hours, missing Andrea and reminiscing about their time together.

He refused to compare Katie to Andrea. They were radically different, and any trip down that road was grossly unfair to both of them—no, to all three of them.

He and Katie were going out Saturday night, he hoped. He felt weird calling it dating. He didn't know what other thirty-seven-year-old men called it. Most of his friends were married or burned badly enough by a failed marriage, and the aftermath, to avoid the whole process.

Pete had tickets for *1968: The Year That Rocked the World* at the Minnesota History Theatre. In 1968 he was just a twinkle in his dad's eye. Five years his junior, in 1968, Katie had yet to achieve even that state of being—or not being.

Being or not being? Wow, he sounded like Shakespeare. Perhaps he should hang up his holster and start writing. Perhaps not. Pete laughed and again shook his head. He'd also never cut it as a comedian.

Just then, a series of alarming sounds threw him back into the present, and wiped away his smile. He heard a racing car or truck engine, followed by screeching tires. The commotion was ahead of him and nearby.

Whenever he heard those sounds, he cringed and held his breath, hoping they weren't followed by the sounds of a crash. The sound of metal or plastic impacting something more or less firm. The sound of breaking glass.

Unfortunately, his wishes didn't halt the events already in motion. He heard the impact. Worse yet, he thought he heard a scream. It sounded like a combination of pain and surprise.

Pete took off, sprinting and saying a silent prayer. He had a cell in his pocket. He thought about slowing down to call 911. He decided against it. He was less than a minute away. He might, God forbid, be able to provide desperately needed assistance before an ambulance could arrive.

Closing the distance between himself and the accident, Pete saw the cause of the commotion. A black Buick LeSabre had slammed into a tree on the median. He couldn't see the driver. He wondered if the driver was thrown out upon impact. Nearing the location, he got a clearer picture.

"Dear God," he gasped.

TWO

Someone was pinned between the LeSabre and an oak. A stocking cap didn't mask the fact it was a man. His body lay slumped over the hood of the Buick.

The sight was gut-wrenching. Pete sprinted the last hundred feet. In the predawn silence, he heard the man's labored breathing. It was a welcomed sound. Even so, he winced, empathizing with the plight of the victim.

Pete bent over the pinned man. His face was within a foot of the other man's, as he stated, "I'm here to help. What's your name?"

The man didn't open his eyes. His face remained relaxed and expressionless. He looked like he was sleeping. He displayed no discernible reaction to Pete's words.

Pete thought the man might be in shock. Did his head slam up against the tree, knocking him out? He hoped the guy was oblivious to the pain that must accompany this type of trauma.

Pulling the cell from his pocket, Pete called 911. He reported his location and described the scene.

St. Paul Fire and Rescue, the Traffic and Accident Division of the Saint Paul Police Department, and some squads were dispatched. Under the circumstances, all were a given.

Relying on past experience, Pete specified three squads. While speaking with the dispatcher, he felt the victim's throat, checking his pulse. It was faint, but seemed regular.

Waiting impatiently for the responders, Pete kept his face close to the pinned man's face. He spoke continuously and scanned, as best he could from that angle, for a more complete picture of the scene.

The driver's-side door of the LeSabre was open. A driver thrown from the vehicle couldn't possibly end up between the car and a tree, could he? That would be one for the books. Still, he didn't feel qualified to rule it out.

If not, where was the driver? Knowing a few inches of fresh snow might have provided an answer to that question, Pete reconsidered his appreciation for the dearth of snow this year.

He contemplated explanations for the collision. Was it an example of the threats posed by inattentive drivers, complicated by a pedestrian in the wrong place at the wrong time? Pete was a cop. He knew there were lots of other possibilities. Did the driver intentionally hit the man? Not necessarily. Someone texting while driving could have hit this man, panicked, and run. That was less pessimistic and, with so little information, also seemed more likely.

Did a kid steal a car to go for a joy ride and lose control of the vehicle? If so, this car seemed an unlikely one to steal. What would make a boat like this the vehicle of choice? Did it belong to some enterprising or delinquent kid's parents?

If the car was stolen, was it taken at this hour because fewer people were awake to see the theft—or the thief? Did the driver live in the vicinity, or drive to the vehicle and switch cars? If the car was parked at the owner's residence, the DVS database and license plates would tell if the collision occurred near the location where the vehicle was typically parked at this hour.

He heard squealing tires just before the sound of the crash. Did that indicate the car was braking or accelerating? He thought it sounded like acceleration. If so, that might signal a deliberate "hit."

Like Pete, the victim wore sweats. Was he, too, a runner? Pete was surprised that the man's clothing was black. Who wore black when walking or running predawn? Dressing that way may it more difficult for a driver to see this man. Was that a key variable in this case?

By all indications, the pinned man would require every ounce of resilience and energy he could muster to stay alive. To help improve the other man's chances, Pete peeled off his sweatshirt and wrapped it carefully around the victim's back and shoulders.

As he did this, a red spot appeared on his light-gray sweatshirt. He had to determine the source. Based on the location of the spot, the left sleeve of the other man's sweatshirt seemed likely.

He touched that sleeve. It was damp. A sniff and a glance at his fingers confirmed it. Blood. Pete found a measure of optimism after determining that the sleeve wasn't soaked with blood.

Pete didn't risk pulling up the sleeve to check the severity of the injury. Instead, as carefully as he could, he wrapped a sleeve of his sweatshirt tightly around the man's left arm. It provided a tourniquet of sorts. Then he carefully ran his right hand across the man's other sleeve. No damp spots.

There were no other visible signs of blood. The man's face was unmarred, and he wasn't bleeding from the mouth.

Pete wondered if the color of the victim's sweatshirt masked some serious bleeding. Blood wasn't flowing onto the hood of the LeSabre or the ground. That added another note of optimism to his assessment of the man's predicament. As best he could tell, bleeding, at least external bleeding wasn't yet a major issue.

Still, he knew internal injuries were a grave concern. He wondered if the tree and the Buick were keeping the man alive, by providing compression and preventing a "bleed out." That was feasible.

Waiting for the ambulance, Pete continued speaking incessantly in calm, measured tones. He sought to comfort and reassure the victim. Unconscious people were thought to hear and be aware of what happened around them. Pete believed it and behaved accordingly.

There was nothing else he could do to help the unresponsive victim. Hence, he concentrated on ways to expedite the freeing of this man, once St. Paul Fire and Rescue arrived.

He checked to see if the keys were in the ignition or the front seat of the LeSabre. During this process, which he accomplished in little more than a minute, Pete minimized his contact with any surfaces and made a mental note of everything he touched. He'd provide that information to the Crime Lab. Failing to do so wouldn't earn him any brownie points with his buddies there.

He wasn't surprised when the keys weren't in the ignition or anywhere else he could see. Concern for the victim kept him from a broader search.

Pete returned to the man and resumed his monologue. He concentrated on the victim's face, hoping for a sign he was heard and understood. In the unfortunate event his voice was the last one this man heard, he did his best to make the transition as peaceful as possible.

"Hang in there, buddy," Pete whispered. "Help is on the way. It won't be long. Just…"

A man flew out of a house on the north side of Wheelock Parkway, yelling, "What the hell?"

"Stay back!" Pete brought the man up short. "This is a crime scene. Don't come any closer."

"Did you call 911?" the man shouted.

Pete didn't have time to answer. The predawn calm was shattered again, this time by the sound of sirens. Glancing at his watch, Pete noted their response took less than three minutes. Notably, this was barely more time than it took an elderly resident to put on his clothes, find his glasses, and open his front door.

A St. Paul squad, followed closely by a second, roared up. Both officers were at his side in seconds. They recognized Pete and asked, "What do you want us to do, Commander?"

Staying at the victim's side, Pete conferred with the uniformed officers. They determined the parameters for a house-to-house canvas of the area. Pete remained with the victim while the uniformed officers carried out their assignment.

The third squad arrived and parked behind the first two, on Wheelock. All three stopped far enough from the crash to avoid impeding rescue vehicles.

Before Pete could work with the third officer to set up the crime scene tape and search for car keys, St. Paul Fire and Rescue sped onto the scene. Flashing lights and intermittent bursts from the sirens announced their approach.

An ambulance was followed by the rescue squad and a fire engine. The ambulance stopped on the side street, in close proximity to the Buick. The rescue squad stopped several yards back. The fire engine pulled over on the parkway to avoid blocking the activities of the other two fire and rescue vehicles.

Two paramedics and two EMTs jumped out of the ambulance, ran to the victim, and began providing life support. They took the man's vital signs continuously and inserted IVs.

While they did this, Pete told them about the man's left arm.

"Yeah, saw your handiwork," a paramedic said. He unwound Pete's sweatshirt and cut the sleeve of the black sweatshirt, revealing lacerations on the man's forearm. The blood on the arm was clotted—or frozen. Bleeding ceased. The paramedic placed a wad of gauze over the injury and wrapped it.

"Where are the car keys?" one of the EMTs asked Pete.

"Haven't the foggiest. Not in the ignition. Didn't see them inside the car. Looked, but not carefully. Had other priorities." Partway through, Pete realized the EMT probably mistook him as the driver.

Another EMT set out a bodyboard with a surgical collar and Medical Anti-Shock Trousers, or MAST, designed to fit from a victim's ankles to just under the ribs. In the event of internal injuries, they could be inflated to apply pressure and help prevent internal bleeding or a bleed out.

"I got here a minute or so after it happened," Pete told the EMT who was setting up the bodyboard. "He was unconscious when I arrived. Is that necessarily bad?"

"No, I think it's likely—based on the position of his body and the location of the car—that his head flipped back and slammed into that tree. If that happened, it might have knocked him out. And, sir, where's your jacket? You must be freezing."

"I only had a sweatshirt, and I wrapped it around the guy. I hoped it would help."

"Him, yes—you, no. It's in the twenties. Grab a warm blanket or two out of the back of the ambulance before you go into hypothermia."

Pete was struggling to stay warm. Upon arriving at the scene, he continuously wriggled his toes and massaged his arms at every opportunity. Even so, he was cold. Damned cold. These temperatures were one thing if he was running and had a sweatshirt. It was another story without the sweatshirt and standing still. He did as instructed, grateful for the respite the blankets offered.

While the ambulance crew tended to the victim, the rescue squad hitched the winch on their vehicle to the LeSabre. They carefully coordinated their actions with the ambulance crew. The goal was to free the pinned man as quickly as possible, while maximizing his chances of survival.

The four-person crew of the fire truck stood nearby, prepared to respond instantaneously, should the Buick catch fire.

Simultaneously, the captain in charge of the ambulance crew sat in the cab of the ambulance. While overseeing the activity, he typed away on a laptop. He documented his team's actions, in preparation for completing the required reports.

As Pete pondered the need for photo documentation of the scene and the best angles, the Traffic and Accident Division team arrived. Thankfully, that spared him from attempting to do an adequate job with one of the cameras the squads carried. The Traffic and Accident Division would reconstruct the accident scene and knew much better than he what was needed.

They checked in with Pete and, before the rescue squad was ready to move the vehicle, succeeded in photographing and videotaping the crime scene and surrounding area. By doing so, they preserved the details of the scene and the location.

At this time, Pete was the best thing they had in the way of a witness. He gave the Traffic and Accident Division a detailed description of what he heard before he arrived and what he saw once here.

The LeSabre would be hauled to the impound lot and kept there for examination by the Crime Lab.

As preparations for freeing the victim continued, an EMT shouted into the man's face, attempting to raise him to consciousness. Her efforts had no discernible effect.

Preparations completed, a paramedic and the EMTs stood at the nose of the LeSabre. They positioned themselves to aid the victim.

The rescue squad tightened the cable.

The captain of the ambulance crew gave the signal.

The ambulance crew responded with practiced skill. They coordinated their efforts, supporting the victim as the car that pinned him was smoothly and speedily pulled away. In seconds, the man was secured to the bodyboard.

The competent team fitted the MAST garment around him and inflated it. They secured the surgical collar. After loading him into the ambulance, they hopped aboard and sped off.

Lights flashed. Sirens were silent as the ambulance dashed east to I-35E. A few quick bursts from distant sirens suggested the ambulance was now either on or entering I-35E.

THREE

The early morning hour sorely constricted the benefits of canvassing the area around an accident scene. One of the two officers handling that assignment was already back at Pete's side.

"No leads," she reported.

Pete asked another officer to determine who owned the black 1991 Buick LeSabre. Thanks to the technology at his fingertips, the officer had an answer at a speed that would have scared George Orwell. The owner lived within a half-mile of where the car still stood, on the median.

Pete directed the two officers to check the owner's residence. Waiting for their report, he maintained control over the scene. Could they be lucky enough to have the owner be the driver? he wondered. Wishing that on the owner was unconscionable. Furthermore, he figured that was about as likely as being struck by lightning in Minnesota in December. Highly unlikely. Could happen.

Getting word to the victim's family was a priority. Pete wondered if the victim carried identification. Judging from his clothing, he might have been running. Was that a bad omen?

Running without an ID was, at best, a bad idea. Yet Pete had friends who refused to bother with the "extra baggage." Mentioning the dangers of being unidentifiable in an emergency prompted comments reflecting an indestructibility mindset. Usually attributed to kids, Pete found the attitude also rampant in people in their thirties—his age group. In fact, he had yet to find an age group younger than the eighties where it didn't reign. Perhaps people operated that way because it would be impossible to function if you believed each next step might land you on a banana peel.

If the victim carried a cell phone, the list of contacts might provide essential information for reaching his family. They deserved an opportunity to be with him. Decisions might be necessary, regarding the use of extraordinary measures. Was the victim still alive? Would he live long enough for anyone to make decisions about his care?

The second officer who canvassed the area returned. He spoke with the man Pete waved off while waiting for the emergency responders. That man heard the crash. "He said that by the time he found his glasses and got to a window, he saw a car smashed into a tree and someone trying to help the pinned man. He complained vociferously about being shooed away when he only wanted to help."

"The woman next door to him heard the crash," the officer continued. "She said the noise woke her up. It took a few minutes for her to figure out what it was, get up her courage, and get to a window. When she looked out the window, she saw you, Commander. She also saw her neighbor run out and stop suddenly when you yelled at him. She was still watching when I got to her door. She knew nothing about the events preceding your arrival, Commander."

No one else he interviewed admitted either hearing the crash, or looking out a window to check on the action after the sounds of the crash.

As the officer completed that report, the two officers who went to the car owner's home returned.

The female officer took the lead. "Commander, we spoke with the vehicle owner. On the way to her home, we got her license information. Found out she's ninety-one. It took her forever to answer the door. She wore a bathrobe and slippers. Seriously, she doesn't move fast enough to have jumped out of the Buick and fled the scene without you seeing her." The officer smiled and shook her head.

"Guess you won't be surprised when I tell you she said she didn't know the car was gone," the officer continued. "She walked around me, out the door, and stood on the front steps, looking for her LeSabre. She asked me who took it. Don't get me wrong. I don't think there's anything wrong with her mind. She was blown away. She didn't know what to think or say."

"And what did you say?" Pete asked.

"I told her that's what we're trying to determine. I asked if anyone, other than her, drives the car. She said she never drives the car. I must've gotten a strange look on my face. She said, 'No, dearie, I'm not crazy. My grandson uses it to take me on errands and to appointments.' The grandson doesn't live with her. I got his name and address. We headed right over. The kid's twenty-two. Don't know how he finds time to take his grandmother all over town, but guess I should be impressed that a kid that age cares enough."

"Anyway, he doesn't live far from his grandmother. The kid, Kevin Douglas, is either a pretty good actor, or we woke him up. He said he was home all night, and he went to bed around eleven. Said he doesn't have anyone to vouch for him. His mother works nights and wasn't home yet. Even though he supposedly just rolled out of bed, he said he was in a hurry. Claimed he has to be to work by seven. He works at the Cambridge Garden Center. I've got all the information here for you, Commander," she said, holding out a piece of paper.

"Kevin Douglas had plenty of time to get home from here," Pete said. "What was he wearing when you saw him?"

"Flannel pajama bottoms and a T-shirt. But he had more than enough time to change before we arrived. Since we stopped at his grandmother's first, he could have crawled all the way home and beat us. Of course, that's assuming he's capable of escaping the accident scene without being seen by you, Commander."

FOUR

Another investigator arrived at the accident scene.

Pete briefed his replacement, turned over the scene, and headed home. He was anxious to clean up and get to headquarters. He wanted to find the bastard who mowed down a man in the middle of winter, and left him there to suffer and die.

Would the investigation be handled by the Traffic and Accident Division or Homicide and Robbery? He knew the balance swung to Traffic and Accident. How far was he willing to go to change that?

Pete began preparing his argument before leaving the scene. He considered the possible role of black ice. This morning's conditions favored its formation. A careful examination of the road in the vicinity of the crash eliminated it as an explanation for the Buick going up and over the curb. Furthermore, there was no evidence the driver attempted to stop the LeSabre before it hit the curb.

The fleeing driver's actions could be attributed to panic. The available information offered nothing to support or contradict that.

Pete had been a cop long enough to realize that truth was often stranger than fiction. On a regular basis, people did the unthinkable for the craziest reasons.

He ran full throttle to his car. Experienced runners like Pete didn't do that. They didn't start out cold, and sprint, especially in the winter. It was about as smart as going on a low-carb diet before running a marathon. Concern over his body temperature superseded caution.

He'd ignored the victim's blood and pulled on his sweatshirt the second it was returned to him by an EMT. The extra layer did little to offset the chill he felt right down to his bones. His inadequate dress and stationary position had persisted too long.

Arriving at his 1960s ranch-style rambler, he untied and stepped out of his shoes just inside the back door. He tossed his sweatshirt in the laundry tub and added cold water, hoping the blood would come out with a good soaking. Andrea taught him that. Pete thought about Andrea as he did this. She died more than two years ago, yet his memories of her remained fresh and laced with sadness.

He stripped off his T-shirt in one swift motion on his way down the hall to the bathroom. It took seconds to remove the rest of his clothes, turn on the water, and hop in the shower.

This had to be the closest thing this side of heaven, he decided as the hot water pounded his body, and steam filled the room. He contemplated extending his standard ten-minute shower to enjoy the damp heat a while longer.

Work took precedence. He turned off the water, towel dried, shaved, and dressed. Then he made two pieces of peanut butter toast and put them in a sandwich bag. He grabbed a warm parka, rather than the overcoat he usually wore, and sped out the door.

Pete typically arrived at headquarters much earlier than this. This morning, he decided to take city streets to avoid the final phase of the stop-more-than-go rush hour traffic on I-35E.

As he'd anticipated, when he walked into headquarters, discussions about the early morning crash dominated the conversation. It didn't surprise Pete when wisecracks about his jacket served as a distraction.

"Heading for the North Pole right after work, Pete? Won't have time to stop home and change?" one investigator asked.

"Naw, he's trying to make some money to offset the extravagant gift he bought his mom for Christmas," said another. "He's spending his lunch break cutting blocks of ice down on the Mississippi. He has a list of Alaskan clients. They're trying to offset the effects of global warming. Isn't that right, Commander?"

"Hell no, your interests are local, aren't they, Pete? Aren't you cutting the ice blocks for the Winter Carnival ice sculptures in Rice Park?"

Pete avoided additional comments and a prolonged discussion by foregoing a comeback. He responded only with a smile and, "Uh huh."

He headed to his office.

After zipping through his report, Pete found the senior commander, the head of the Homicide and Robbery Unit, in his office. Prior to the name change, a senior commander was a captain, and Pete, a commander, had the rank of lieutenant.

Pete gave Commander Lincoln his report. Then he recited the *Reader's Digest* version of the crime scene and his activities.

Lincoln told him the victim was at Regions Hospital. He said the man was in the emergency room, and the technical trauma team was still working on him.

"I spoke with a member of that team," Lincoln said. "The guy seems short on luck this morning, aside from the fact he was struck so close to a Level I Trauma Center."

Glancing back and forth between Pete and a page on his desk, Lincoln described the victim's condition. "He sustained compound fractures of his left and right thigh along with multiple lacerations. More significantly, he has a subarachnoid hemorrhage. There's bleeding in the area between the brain and the thin tissues that cover the brain. He's in critical condition. He didn't regain consciousness before they placed him in a medically induced coma to protect his brain from additional stress and damage."

Pete winced.

"I agree," Lincoln said, nodding.

"What did they say about his chances?" Pete asked.

"They're doing tests. I understand the outlook is dismal. By the way, the victim wasn't carrying any identification or a cell."

"I have the initial reconstruction from Traffic and Accident," Lincoln continued. "The LeSabre was traveling north when it approached the intersection just west of the collision. A patch nine feet south of that intersection indicates fresh marks left by spinning tires. A sample of the rubber from those marks is being tested to determine if it matches the LeSabre's tires."

"The LeSabre crossed the eastbound lane of Wheelock Parkway. It hit the curb, blowing both front tires and sending it airborne. Based on the distance the Buick traveled while airborne and the length of the skid marks the blown front tires made on the median, the LeSabre was traveling well over the speed limit when it struck the curb."

"One of the victim's shoes came off at the time of impact," Lincoln said. "The location of that shoe, and the place where the blown tires began leaving marks on the median, suggest the vehicle hit the ground before it struck the victim. The impact injuries reported by the Regions trauma team, which are from shin to upper thigh, support that conclusion. The information from Traffic and Accident will, of course, be fine-tuned in the supplemental reports."

"I want this case, Commander," Pete said.

"Traffic and Accident is already working it."

"And I was working it before they got involved."

"You're going to have to make a better case than that. I see no sense in trying to edge out Traffic and Accident."

"Please hear me out, Commander." Pete silently counted to ten while, as surreptitiously as possible, taking a deep breath.

"Currently, it looks like the LeSabre was stolen," he began. "According to the information compiled thus far by the Traffic and Accident Division, the driver made no effort to stop the vehicle before the car went airborne. By all indications, this qualifies, minimally, as an assault, and more likely as an aggravated assault. Homicide handles those cases, not Traffic and Accident. I'm the closest thing we have to a witness. I was the first member of the unit at the scene. I handled the scene during the initial phases. I *want* this case."

"Okay, it's yours; but only because you're so adamant, Pete," Lincoln sighed. "I'll assign you as the lead investigator. Martin Tierney will work the case with you."

"Thanks, Commander."

Lincoln nodded.

Pete didn't have to go far before bumping into Martin Tierney, the junior partner in this duo. Martin's lower rank, detective sergeant versus commander, reflected both the differences in experience and expertise. Martin hoped to eliminate those disparities ASAP.

Other differences he'd like to eliminate were largely beyond his control. Martin was jealous of the six inches Pete towered over him, and he envied Pete's thick hair and thin physique. Although he might have had more control over that last item, to date he lacked the willpower.

Pete contacted the trauma team and checked on the possibility of obtaining the victim's fingerprints.

After the trauma team determined it wouldn't endanger him, the victim was fingerprinted. His fingerprints were run through AFIS, the Automated Fingerprint Identification System. There were no matches. That meant the victim hadn't served in the military, hadn't been arrested, and didn't have a security clearance. It did nothing else to help identify him.

With no leads for determining the vehicle driver and no identification for the victim, the options for solving this case were limited. The two investigators pursued every available avenue for obtaining the victim's identity.

Pete contacted the department's public information staff. He provided the information required to assemble a blurb for the morning newscasts at eleven and eleven thirty, and again at noon. It would include a description of the victim, his apparel, and the location of the accident. If nothing happened between now and those broadcasts, the announcements could be a key resource.

Meanwhile, Martin checked with the communication office. He was interested in any calls that didn't qualify for missing person reports, but involved someone who'd gone missing between five and seven that morning. He gave them information to narrow the field, and asked to be notified of anything that met the victim's description and the location of the accident.

Pete and Martin considered other possible avenues. They would start by establishing the vehicle owner's credibility when it came to her noninvolvement. Then they'd investigate her grandson. Between the two they hoped to develop some leads.

They were preparing to leave headquarters when the senior commander notified Pete of a call to Regions Hospital from a woman looking for her husband. The description she provided was a forty-two-year-old man, five-eight, about 155 pounds. Her husband had brown hair and brown eyes. She said his only scar was U-shaped and on the inside of his left wrist. She provided a home address located a block north of Wheelock Parkway and near the Gateway Trail.

The man's name was Nicholas Rice. His wife, Heather, told Regions he hadn't returned from his daily run. She wasn't sure what time he left that morning, but he should have been home before seven o'clock.

Through tears, she explained that she checked the garage. His car was there, and she'd found his ID in the driveway. She was convinced something had happened. She was afraid he'd collapsed and needed medical attention. She called Regions, while frantically checking with all of the hospitals in the vicinity of their home.

FIVE

Pete phoned Heather Rice—the woman who called Regions Hospital, looking for her husband. It seemed likely she was the victim's wife. Her descriptions of her husband and what he wore when running were a perfect match.

Pete minimized the conversation. He hoped the man was her husband. More altruistically, he hoped the man was alive when Heather reached his side. In an effort to improve the chances, he provided only the name of the hospital and the victim's condition.

If the man was Heather's husband, Pete had a lot of questions for her. Those questions weren't, shouldn't be, the top priority at a time like this.

The two investigators raced to Regions. They would wait in the wings until Mrs. Rice had an opportunity to identify the man.

But Pete and Martin didn't put all their money in one stock. While they were at Regions, other efforts they orchestrated to identify the victim continued.

Assuming the man was her husband, Pete hoped the victim could communicate with her. He knew how it felt to have a loved one snatched from your life without warning. That's what happened with his wife. A drunk driver broadsided Andrea's car. She died instantly. He couldn't tell her one last time how much he loved her. Sure, she knew. Knowing that provided little consolation. At times like this, the wound felt fresh. His pain rose to the surface.

Pete didn't share these thoughts with Martin. He didn't need to.

Martin keyed in on the change in Pete. He knew about Andrea's death, and drew the correct conclusions. He thought about taking

Pete's mind off the past by diving into a discussion of the case or some small talk. He decided against it.

Would this event affect Pete's relationship with Katie Benton? Martin wondered. It took Pete a long time to move far enough from Andrea's death to begin dating. Would this event create a new barrier? Would it doom Pete's relationship with Katie?

Martin wished Pete hadn't heard the crash and arrived so quickly. That might have added to Pete's pain. Martin had done his best to bug, cajole, and coerce Pete to re-immerse himself in the dating world. He hoped all of those efforts, and Pete's, wouldn't be undone in a single day—a single morning.

On the way to Regions, Pete did a quick calculation. If Heather Rice left home as soon as she hung up, and didn't speed, it would take her about fifteen minutes to reach Regions. In a case like this, getting to her destination probably superceded obeying the rules of the road. Regions had valet parking. She'd probably use it to save time. She sounded frantic when he spoke with her.

Would the failure to use valet parking smack of indifference? If so, was she the driver of the car that struck her husband? If not, how much could she help their investigation?

While Martin parked the car, Pete called the emergency room. He explained who he was and asked for the current location of the unidentified man brought in this morning. He breathed a sigh of relief when the staff member recited one. The victim was in the Intensive Care Unit—not the morgue.

On the elevator to the ICU, Pete shared his plan with Martin.

A minute later, Martin positioned himself down the hall from the victim's room. He selected a spot that gave him a clear view of that hospital room door. He wanted to know the second Heather Rice arrived.

Pete stopped at the nurses' station. He asked for a status report on the victim, now presumed to be Nicholas Rice. A badge worked wonders in a case like this. The nurse transitioned from uncooperative to helpful in a fraction of a second.

The news wasn't good. The victim was dependent upon life support and remained in a medically induced coma. They were doing everything possible to keep him alive. When Pete asked the likelihood of the man's survival, the nurse shook her head and shrugged. "It happens, but..."

A woman ran to the nurses' station, interrupting that assessment. The look on the woman's face indicated she was Heather Rice, or had received comparable news about a loved one. Her lips were pursed. Her eyes were moist. Her nose was red.

She was out of breath, and explained between gasps that the police called her. She said she was looking for the unidentified man in the unit. She was sure he was her husband.

The nurse led the woman to the door under surveillance by Martin.

Pete joined Martin and told him what the nurse said about the victim.

Martin frowned and shook his head.

Waiting for confirmation that Heather Rice was the victim's spouse, Pete noticed the sounds of the ICU. He was surprised by the level of noise emitted by monitoring devices and who knew what else? He felt confident that the incessant clicks and beeps would drive him to distraction in no time flat. Add the medicinal smells and, in his opinion, the hospital—at least this wing of the hospital—was an unappealing place to spend much time.

If someone dear was on the receiving end of the efforts underway here, he realized, it was unlikely the sounds and smells were a consideration.

The two investigators waited. Patience was mandatory. If the victim was Nicholas Rice, Heather was the best starting point. If she wouldn't be available for a prolonged period, he and Martin would split up. One would stay here. The other would begin talking with other members of the Rice family and the family's neighbors.

Martin glanced at his watch as surreptitiously as possible. He, too, thought about how long they might have to wait. He believed that in all likelihood the victim was Rice. If so, Rice was unconscious. Would that increase or decrease the wait?

Would Pete interrupt Heather Rice's time with her husband, knowing it might be their final moments together? Would a home run hitter return to the dugout without stepping on home plate? That was just slightly more likely.

The nurse exited the room, alone, and approached Pete and Martin, interrupting Martin's analysis.

SIX

"The patient is her husband. He's Nicholas Rice," the nurse told Pete and Martin. "I explained his status. She's functioning somewhere between disbelief and denial. She wants to talk to the doctor. She also wants to know about bringing their children to see him. She's torn over whether or not that's a good idea. They're twelve, ten, and eight."

"Ouch," Pete and Martin whispered simultaneously.

"Glad I'm not her," the nurse continued. "I think it depends on the kids. They may be old enough to decide for themselves."

After the nurse walked away, Pete stepped to the door of Nicholas Rice's room. Hoping to avoid an untimely interruption, he looked in before knocking gently.

In response to Pete's knock, Heather Rice set her husband's hand on the bed. She brushed a few strands of hair from his brow, bent over him, and kissed his forehead. Then she smiled weakly at him and walked to the door.

She was tall and looked like she'd spent time with a personal trainer. Her ultrashort blonde hair was styled for wash and wear. Her blue eyes were swollen, and her nose was redder than when Pete saw her, minutes earlier. She wore an expensive-looking, brown wool suit. The brightly colored scarf around her neck contradicted her expression, and the atmosphere in the room. She clutched a wad of tissues in her left hand.

Stepping into the hallway, she asked in a quavering voice, "Are you Nick's doctor?"

Pete saw she struggled to maintain control.

"No. We're sorry to bother you at a time like this. I'm Peter Culnane. I'm with the St. Paul Police Department. I spoke with you earlier." Tilting his head in Martin's direction, Pete added, "This is my partner, Martin Tierney."

Heather nodded and reached for Pete's hand. "I don't know how I can thank you enough—you and your department. When I got the paper this morning, I found Nick's license in the driveway. I didn't think anything of it, until he didn't return from his run. I started calling hospitals."

"We'll do everything possible to find the person who did this, Mrs. Rice. If you'll take a few minutes now to answer our questions, it'll help us with the investigation."

"What kind of questions? And please, call me Heather."

They moved into Nick's room and continued the discussion.

Nicholas Rice was handsome. He looked younger than Heather, younger than forty-two. Pete wondered if that meant his life was smooth sailing prior to this morning. The man looked peaceful. That had to be of comfort to his wife. The wounds on his legs were hidden by the sheet and the hospital gown. The only sign of injury was a bandage around his left arm.

"Currently, we have nothing to indicate this was anything but an accident," Pete said. "Even so, we have to ask some questions to help us rule out the possibility it was intentional."

"How could it be intentional? Why would anyone want to do this to Nick? He doesn't have any enemies." Heather was adamant.

Pete asked if her husband acted differently in the last few days, weeks, or months.

Heather said he'd been less predictable and seemed more nervous. She'd attributed it to their daughter's emotional problems. This past fall was a difficult time for all of them, she explained. Heather broke down while telling Pete and Martin about their daughter's ongoing problems with school.

"I don't know how we're going to get through this. We all depend on Nick for emotional support, and Alexis and Nick have a special bond. She's our only daughter, and there's often a special bond between girls and their dads, you know. Poor Alexis. I don't know if she'll be able to handle seeing Nick this way."

Through a series of questions, Pete and Martin obtained a list of Nick's friends. Heather recited the names and contact information for their family members on her side and Nick's. Then she gave the name and location of Nick's employer, Regisson Medical.

When another man walked in, interrupting their discussion, Pete obtained Heather's cell phone number and cut short their meeting.

The two investigators decided to start by talking to Rice's coworkers at Regisson Medical. Per Heather, two of her husband's best friends worked there.

Located in Woodbury, an eastern suburb of St. Paul, Regisson Medical appeared to anticipate significant expansion. The five-story office building stood isolated from nearby development. A park spread over several wooded acres and surrounded the office building.

The two investigators walked through the front door and into a two-story, glass-fronted reception area. The furnishings conveyed the impression of a successful, fledgling company, or an older establishment with a sudden influx of bucks.

Pete identified himself, and asked the receptionist for an organizational chart that included names and titles. Judging from her reaction, you'd think he asked to use the CEO's private privy.

He didn't intend to begin with the office manager. It became necessary in order to get the organizational chart.

Chart in hand, Pete and Martin made their way through the office building. They identified themselves and talked to everyone they could find.

Starting at the top, they met with the CEO. He was shocked to hear about Nicholas Rice's accident. He said only good things about Rice. Said Rice loved challenges, was a terrific problem solver, avoided confrontation. He wasn't aware of any problems in Rice's life, or any enemies.

Repeatedly, their news was met with surprise and disbelief. They heard that Rice was a nice guy, a hard worker, analytical, enthusiastic, loved complexity and challenges, hated humdrum, played nicely with others, and had nary an enemy.

One person's description varied from that path. This man, Mike Washington, was one of Rice's subordinates. He described Rice much as everyone else had, then added a new wrinkle. He said Rice was always working "to expand his kingdom."

When asked for clarification, he said, "Nick is always looking for new projects, new activities, new challenges. That's fine, I guess. It gives us job security, but we aren't adding staff. And he could care less how we've done it for years. He's always finding 'a better way.'"

"In other words, he's a demanding task master," Pete said.

"I guess it sounds that way, but he's easy to work for. I mean, he doesn't get on our backs. He doesn't micromanage. He's always supportive."

"How long have you worked for Rice?" Pete asked.

"A couple of years. I was here before he came to Regisson and before he became a VP."

"Did that irritate you, I mean Rice getting the VP job?" Pete asked.

"No."

"Did you apply for it?" Pete asked.

"No. I didn't want the job. I don't thrive on pressure the way some people do. I like what I'm doing."

"Did you like it better before Rice became your boss?" Pete asked.

"Sure."

"A guy like Rice can take the fun out of a job, can't he?" Martin probed.

"Sometimes."

"A guy like Nick doesn't usually stay in one job very long. That type of person usually has a master plan for his career. Do you agree?" Martin asked.

"Sounds reasonable. You can also bet it's a bad idea to let your employer know if your current job is nothing more than a stepping stone," Washington said, accentuating it with a knowing look.

"I'd guess some of the stressors in your life will evaporate, once Rice moves along," Pete said.

"Not necessarily. That's a two-sided coin."

"But a guy like Rice can test your patience, drive you over the edge, can't he?" Martin continued.

"And sometimes you just accept it, collect your paycheck, and thank God you have a job in an economy like this. No, I didn't do it. I'm not that chickenshit," Washington said, slamming his hand on his desk. "Whenever I have a beef with Nick, I tell him. I wouldn't try to mow him down like a weed. He has a wife and three young kids."

Washington closed his eyes and shook his head. "Nick is like a cheerleader around here. He must be that way at home, too. I wonder what they'd do without him. Hope they don't have to find out."

"Stress is an integral part of Nick Rice's job?" Pete asked.

"You'd better believe it!"

"Did Rice thrive on stress?" Pete asked.

"He must've."

"Did he show signs of stress in the last few days, weeks, or months?" Pete asked.

"Well, I guess he was a bit edgier, a bit more distracted."

"Can you attribute that to anything in particular?" Pete asked.

"I don't know. There's nothing unusual going on that I'm aware of, but I have no idea what's happening at Nick's level. He isn't likely to share that with me."

"Who does Nick hang out with around here? Does he eat with any particular group or individuals? Does he socialize with anyone who works here?" Pete asked.

"He used to go out to lunch with Brian Traverse and Pat Steele almost every day."

Pete recognized both names. They were on the list of friends provided by Heather Rice. He hadn't placed a checkmark by the second name. Steele wasn't in the office—at least not when he and Martin last checked.

"Used to?" Pete asked.

"Yeah, he's been eating here, in the lunchroom, a lot lately."

"Any idea why he'd start doing that?" Pete asked.

"Nope."

"Did he say anything about trying to save money, cut expenses, anything like that?" Pete asked.

"Come on, he'd never have that discussion with someone at my level."

Pete and Martin each handed Washington one of their business cards and asked him to call if he thought of anything that might assist with their investigation.

"I might be able to do that if you tell me what you're looking for."

"Any information on what's been making Rice more nervous, any thoughts on problems he was having, any discussion about Rice by your coworkers that surprises you, anything like that. I'm confident you've got the idea," Pete said.

"In other words, you're asking me to rat out my coworkers?"

"I'm sure you want to see that justice is done for the sake of Nick and his family," Pete said.

Pete wanted to get back to Brian Traverse and check on Steele's whereabouts. When he looked at his watch, it was four fifty-five. Covering two bases at once, Martin went to ask the receptionist about Steele, while Pete searched for Traverse.

SEVEN

Martin reached the receptionist's desk in time to see her shut down her computer. While he stood there, waiting to be acknowledged, she continued preparing to depart. He didn't think she was ignoring him. She appeared to be oblivious to his presence.

He resorted to interrupting her efforts by saying, "Excuse me, I have a couple of questions."

She glanced at her watch, rolled her eyes, and sighed.

Hoping to elicit her cooperation, Martin said, "Sorry if I'm holding you up. This is important and can't wait until tomorrow. I only need a minute," he said without pausing. "First, can you tell me if Pat Steele is in? He wasn't here when my partner and I arrived."

She pointed to the sign-out board and recited it for him. "Pat will be back tomorrow afternoon, barring any unforeseen circumstances, that is. He's often held up by unexpected problems. If I were you, I'd call first." She fidgeted and squirmed throughout this recital.

Martin thanked her and asked for Steele's phone number.

She removed a glove, wrote the number on a Post-it note and handed it to him. "Can I go now?" she asked.

"One more thing. I understand that Nicholas Rice began eating his lunches here, rather than going out to lunch. Are you aware of that?"

"Yes."

"Did he or anyone else say why he was doing that?"

"No, and I thought you only had one more question."

"I do." Martin smiled, hoping to maintain her cooperation. "About how long has he been doing that?"

She bit her lip and gazed down, fixating on the floor, "I'd say since right after the first of the year. I don't remember him eating here before or during the holidays. Yeah, I think he started doing that after the first of the year."

"Here's my business card," Martin said, holding it out. "Please don't hesitate to call if you think of anything that might help with our investigation. Solving the case will make the difficult road his family is on a little less bumpy."

Martin's comment must have struck a chord. She reached for the card, smiled, and said, "Sorry I've been such a pain. When I'm late, the driver in my carpool gets nasty. I'll do as you ask. My heart's breaking for Heather and the kids, especially Alexis. She worships her dad. If you're finished, Mister—," she glanced down at the business card in her hand, "—Tierney, I'd better get going."

Assignment accomplished, Martin thanked her and searched for Pete.

Meanwhile, for the second time this morning, Pete found Brian Traverse in his office. This time, he wanted to know if Traverse's failure to note changes in Rice's behavior or patterns represented an innocent mistake, an oversight explained by unexpected news about Rice, something equally innocuous or...

Out of deference, Pete stood outside Traverse's office, waiting for Rice's friend to complete an animated telephone conversation.

For a surprisingly long time, Traverse failed to notice Pete. He sat at his desk. His left hand was clenched in a fist that covered his mouth. He concentrated on a tablet, writing, drawing, or scribbling on it.

Seeing Pete, he held up an index finger and mouthed "one minute." At the same time, he slid a stack of pages over the tablet.

Until a moment ago, Pete figured, he could have seen what Traverse was working on—if he was seven feet tall. He wasn't, and he couldn't. He wondered if the stacks of paper and other items on

Traverse's desk had coincidentally or intentionally prohibited it. He made a mental note.

Traverse turned his back to Pete and hung up the phone. Then he walked to the door. He extended a hand, and Pete noted the strength of his grip. When he commented on it, Traverse reddened and attributed it to four years on his college's crew team.

Traverse remained seated the last time Pete spoke with him. Now, standing beside him, Pete got a better view of the other man. Brian Traverse was tall, had a wiry build, and sandy blond hair.

Once they were seated, Pete began. "Glad you're still here. Thought of a few more questions."

"Oh? Namely?"

"Some of your coworkers said Nick has been different in the last while. You failed to mention that. Care to reconsider?" Pete asked.

"You have to be more specific."

"Did you see any changes in his habits, his schedule, his personality?"

"He's been nervous, but not so much so that I was concerned. I didn't think it needed mentioning. You know, the demands of the holiday season. We all tend to be more stressed, more exhausted."

"I understand he started eating lunch here, rather than catching a bite with you and Pat Steele."

"Yeah, he said he went a little crazy with Christmas gifts. Had to save some money."

"When did he start eating here?" Pete asked.

"I'm not sure. Probably a little before or a little after Christmas."

"Say the vehicle that hit Nick struck him intentionally. If he suspected something, he may have mentioned it to a close friend. I thought you might have heard something," Pete said.

"Nick never said anything like that. He once mentioned that his sister suspected someone was stalking her. Pat and I razzed him about it. Pat said, 'Yeah, doctor, my best friend has this horrible itch he can't get rid of...'"

"How did Nick react to that?" Pete asked.

"He laughed and said he'd tell his sister to go to the doctor herself."

"After that, did he drop it?"

"Not before he convinced us he wasn't talking about himself and asked us what we'd do if she was our sister. He's a great debater. Must've been in debate club in school. By the time he finished, I was sure it was his sister's problem."

"Did you have any recommendations?" Pete asked.

"A few."

"Namely?"

"Pack up and leave town in the middle of the night. Call the police. From there it went south. We told him his sister should join the witness protection program, dye her hair, have plastic surgery— every stupid idea that came to us."

Martin joined Pete in time to hear the last remark.

"How did Nick react to your recommendations?" Pete asked.

"He said his sister would appreciate the help, and he changed the subject."

"Was he ticked?" Pete asked.

"If he was, he didn't show it. In retrospect, looks like he was talking about himself after all." Traverse looked repentant.

"Am I correct in assuming that a company like Regisson thrives on new patents?" Pete asked.

"Absolutely!"

"Are you, Nick, and others at your level privy to these discoveries before they are patented?"

"Some of us, of course. Who knows depends on the divisions involved. There'd be hell to pay if you shared the information."

"Seems unlikely any of those developments are in, or linked to, Nick Rice's area," Pete said.

"You'd be surprised. These things usually cross departments."

"Is Regisson preparing for another rollout?" Pete asked.

"That's the word. No one is saying anything, but I can usually feel it in the air."

"Did Nick say anything to you about it?" Pete asked.

"Only that he knew something was on the horizon."

"That's all for now," Pete said. "You can help by contacting one of us if you remember anything that bears even a remote relationship to our conversation, or if you hear any conversations that might be of interest."

"You suspect someone around here?" Traverse asked.

"For now, we suspect no one in particular and everyone in general," Pete said.

As they left Regisson Medical, Martin asked, "What did I miss?"

"Nick told Traverse and Steele that his sister thought someone was tailing her."

"And based on what happened this morning, that probably means Rice thought someone was tailing him," Martin said. "Why wouldn't he tell them he was worried about himself, rather than his sister?"

"We can only assume that. It's possible he was worried about his sister. In an effort to help, he could have gotten in the middle of her situation and become another target."

EIGHT

L et's find Rice's sister," Pete told Martin. Thinking out loud, he
added, "I wonder if the man who interrupted our conversation with
Heather Rice was her husband's doctor. If there was a significant change
in Rice's condition," he added, "the hospital would have updated us."

"No news is good news," Martin said.

Pete retrieved his trusty three-by-five-inch notepad from the
inside pocket of his suit coat. His nephew thought it archaic that he
still kept some of his notes on paper. He didn't care. He remembered
names better when he wrote them by hand. Almost as important, he
refused to depend completely on a device that relied on a battery and
was subject to failure.

No matter how many times he dropped his notepad, his jottings
remained accessible. Dropping it in a puddle complicated the retrieval,
but didn't flip his notes into a black hole.

He didn't know of a single investigator, from the youngest to
the oldest, who relied solely on an electronic device for all of their
important data.

Pete found and dialed the cell phone number Heather provided
for Sarah Houston, Nicholas Rice's sister. Voicemail answered. He
left a message, tipping off Martin to his failure to reach Sarah.

"She might be at the hospital," Martin offered.

"True, but cell phones can now be used in hospitals. Even so,
guess she might not want to be bothered right now. It could be a very
solemn or somber moment."

"Yeah," Martin sighed.

During their second trip to Regions, Martin shared some news.
"Haven't had a chance to tell you, Pete. Michelle's pregnant. We're
thrilled!"

Martin could have foregone the last statement. Pete knew that Martin and Michelle had spent years trying to expand their family. Besides, Martin's expression broadcast his happiness.

"Congratulations, Martin. That's fantastic!"

"Yeah, I was beginning to think Marty would never have a sibling. I have to tell you, trying to have a kid has to rank as the best way to take the pleasure out of sex. Hey, speaking of that, what's happening with you and Katie Benton?"

"We get together once a week or so—when my schedule permits."

"And?"

"And so far she's putting up with my schedule and me. After five months, I'm happy with our relationship."

"Are you thinking about the future?"

"Not yet. It's too soon, if for no other reason than I don't want to scare her off. How about your future, Martin? When's the baby due?"

"We think early July. Michelle's having an ultrasound today. I might find out the baby's sex tonight. Can't wait to hear!"

"Martin, you could have a 'Yankee Doodle Dandy.'"

"I prefer a baby."

"I'm referring to 'I'm A Yankee Doodle Dandy' by George M. Cohan." Pete sang the chorus. *"I'm A Yankee Doodle Dandy... born on the Fourth of July...* Now do you know what I mean?"

"Yes. We'll have a Yankee Doodle Dandy if the baby is born on July fourth. Thanks, Perry."

"Wait a minute. You're familiar with Perry Como and not George M. Cohan?"

"Ask Michelle." Martin laughed. "She often accuses me of having selective hearing."

"Getting back to the baby, do you have a preference, a boy or a girl, Martin?"

"No way. I'm curious, but I'm so thrilled, I really don't care. I just want the kid to be healthy."

NINE

Nick Rice's sister wasn't in his room.

Heather sat at his bedside, holding his hand. Her head rested on his pillow, as she stared at his face. Every few seconds, a tear rolled down her cheek, dropping silently on the bed.

As if she understood the question on the minds of both investigators, Heather said, "No change. I spoke with a member of the trauma team. I had to press to get him to tell me Nick's chances. Finally, he said he has about a forty percent chance of surviving. He said if he does make it, Nick will have short-term memory problems and have to undergo lots of physical and occupational therapy. He may never again be the Nick we know," she wept.

Through sobs, she continued, "I don't care. I just want him to make it. That's all that matters. I'm trying to bring in another neurologist, but there are problems with using the one I want. It has to do with his not practicing at this hospital. I'm trying to circumvent that limitation. Don't get me wrong. I know Nick's getting excellent care. Still, I want an outside opinion. Don't you think that's fair? These roadblocks are so frustrating."

"I also spoke with a friend who is a psychologist," Heather went on. "I wanted to make sure I don't hurt the children by bringing them to see their dad. I was told I should allow them to decide. The boys seem so young, and I was afraid Alexis might feel pressured to come if they wanted to. That's why it's taken so long."

"All three want to see their dad," she said finally. "Nick's sister, Sarah, is picking them up. They should be here shortly. I've been praying all day that Nick lives and that the kids aren't scarred by all this. I'm also praying we all heal—completely."

She didn't look confident that would happen. It was obvious from her face and the slump of her shoulders that it had been a long and devastating day.

"Our hearts go out to you, Heather," Pete said. "We'd like to stick close and speak with Nick's sister. We're willing to wait. Just so you know, it shouldn't take long. At this point, we have only a few questions for her."

Heather nodded and asked, "Are you willing to wait long enough for Sarah to spend a few minutes here with the kids and me?"

Pete nodded.

"Thanks. After that, I'll ask her to look for you. Where will you be?"

"Down the hall, by the first bank of elevators," Pete said.

The two investigators left Heather and her husband. They found an inconspicuous spot where they could see the elevators and Nick's room.

It wasn't long before a woman with three young children exited an elevator and passed them. By all appearances, this was the family of Nick Rice. The woman and children seemed unaware of the two investigators.

All four looked panic-stricken and shell-shocked. The woman bore no apparent resemblance to Nick. If she was five feet tall, it was barely.

The young girl resembled Heather. She clung to the woman's hand with both of hers and held it tight against her cheek. Her tears flowed, unchecked.

The older boy had an arm firmly around the smaller boy's shoulder. He bit his lower lip so hard, it was white. He was the spitting image of Nick Rice, from his facial features right down to his hairline and hair color.

The younger boy had his face buried in the sleeve of the older boy's jacket. Not an inch of it was visible, but his hair was the same color as the other boy's.

After they passed, Martin leaned up against the wall and crossed his arms over his chest.

Pete burned off nervous energy by pacing back and forth down the hallway.

Martin listened to the sound of Pete's footsteps on the linoleum. He'd recognize Pete's distinct and measured gait anywhere. It exuded confidence and self-assurance.

Pete was anxious to keep the investigation moving. He also wanted to speak with Nick's brother and Rice's neighbors before hanging it up for the day.

Interspersed with thoughts about the investigation, he wondered how Martin would react to another day that never ended. He understood. Martin had a family and the requisite obligations.

How about Katie Benton? Would she be patient when he needed to reach closure on an investigation?

Before long, Sarah Houston left her brother's room and approached Pete and Martin.

TEN

Extending a hand to first Pete, then Martin, Sarah introduced herself.

Pete noticed that her hand was ice cold. "We have a few questions," he said. "Let's find a more comfortable location. Would you like something to eat or drink, Sarah?"

"No, and I prefer to stay close by. Do you know if there's anything in the vicinity?"

The three of them walked to the nurses' station. A nurse directed them to an empty room not far from the one occupied by Nick and his family.

Once seated, Pete said, "As I told Heather, at this point, we don't know if Nick was struck accidentally or on purpose. We're asking a lot of questions, attacking this investigation from every conceivable angle. If it was intentional, the person who struck him might have spent time before today, following him, determining his habits. Did Nick ever say anything, suggesting he thought he was being followed?"

"No. Why didn't he tell me? He should have told me!" Sarah's reaction brought the first signs of life to her face.

"You're jumping to conclusions, Sarah. Remember, we don't know this was anything but an accident. So, Nick never implied he was being followed, even jokingly?" Pete asked.

"Not to me."

"If he suspected it was happening, do you think he'd tell you?" Pete asked.

"There's maybe a fifty-fifty chance. He tells me some things, but who tells everything to anyone? Even if he thought it was happening, he may not have said anything. There could be a dozen reasons why. It's possible he didn't want to scare me."

"Would you tell Nick if you thought you were being followed?" Martin asked.

"I don't know. I wouldn't want him to worry about me, but he'd be hurt and furious if I thought it was happening to me and didn't tell him. I suppose I'd tell him."

"Have you ever suspected you were being followed?" Martin asked.

"Gratefully, no," Sarah said with a sigh. "Are we almost finished? I want to get back to Heather and the kids."

"We only need a few more minutes," Pete said. "Did you see much of Nick in the last month or two?"

"I saw him on Christmas Day at Dad's house. Haven't seen him since."

"Was there anything different about him at that time?" Pete asked.

"I'm not sure I understand the question."

"Was he unusually nervous, irritable, apprehensive? Anything that wasn't normal for him?" Pete said.

"It was Christmas. The kids were wired. Not just his. Mine, too. I don't know if it was all the cookies they ate, the pop they drank, or all the presents. Might have been a combination of all three. Nick thought it was hilarious. It seemed like every time I got them calmed down, he stirred them up. On purpose. I think he was having as much fun as the kids—maybe more." A faint smile crossed her lips. It might have been triggered by the memories.

"And that was the last time you saw him?" Pete asked.

"Yes. We both have families. Our kids have more activities in a week than I had in a month when I was in grade school."

"Are Nick and your other brother close?" Pete asked.

"Nick and Cory are like Holmes and Watson, Butch Cassidy and the Sundance Kid, the 'two' Musketeers."

"You seem to have covered the range of possibilities, at least from a cop's perspective." Pete smiled. "Are you expecting Cory? Heather said he's in Canada. Edmonton, Alberta, correct?"

"Cory's in Fort McMurray right now. It's about a six-hour drive from Edmonton. I spoke with him a couple of hours ago. He'll be here sometime tonight."

"Fort McMurray? He lives there?" Pete asked.

"Yes, well, both there and Edmonton. The oil company he works for provides company housing while he's in Fort McMurray. The company also flies him back and forth from there to Edmonton. He has an apartment in Edmonton. Said he'd go stir-crazy if he spent all his time in Fort McMurray."

"How long has he been there?" Pete asked.

"A couple of years. He's a safety engineer on the tar sands around Fort McMurray."

"How did he end up in Canada? Did the economy drive him north?" Pete asked.

"Cory was recruited by a headhunter. It was an attractive offer. He makes a load of money."

"How about your dad?" Pete asked.

"Dad's too sick to come see Nick. He came down with viral pneumonia several days ago. I checked. They won't let anyone who is sick visit anyone in intensive care. I was told it's too dangerous for the patients. They're real sticklers about that. Wish I hadn't asked. Dad could have worn a face mask or something. He wants to be with Nick." Sarah struggled to get the words out, as mascara left tracks down her cheeks. She pulled a tissue from her purse, dabbed her face and eyes, and blew her nose. "Sorry. I can't help it. I'm not sure Dad will survive if Nick dies, and he isn't able to see him first. Actually, I'm not sure he'll survive this, either way."

"My heart goes out to you—to your whole family," Pete said. "Please bear with us. We only have a few more questions. You and Heather both mentioned your father. Hope I'm not touching on a sensitive subject when I ask about your mother."

"No, that's okay. She packed up and moved to Texas when Nick, Cory, and I were teenagers. We hear from her at Christmas, but haven't seen her in eight or nine years."

"Can you think of anyone who might want to hurt Nick—anyone who could have a grudge against him?" Pete asked.

"No. Nick has a lot of friends. I can't remember the last time I saw him argue with anyone. It may have been when he was in grade school. Honestly, I can't imagine this being intentional. Are you sure it was?"

"No, thus far, we have no reason to conclude it was. As my partner mentioned, at this point we're looking at every possibility," Martin said.

"Could Heather and the kids be in danger?"

"We have no reason to believe they are," Martin said.

"And no reason to believe they aren't?" Sarah challenged.

After giving Pete an opportunity to jump in and field that question, Martin said, "You said you don't believe what happened was intentional. We've heard nothing from you or Heather to indicate it was. If we learn of a reason to be concerned, we'll act."

Sarah crossed her arms, sighed deeply, shook her head, and said, "That does little to reassure me."

"That statement leads me to believe you're convinced that what happened was intentional. Are you?" Pete asked.

Sarah sighed again and said, "Well, I guess I'm feeling a little paranoid."

On their way to the parking ramp, Martin asked Pete, "Okay, explain it to me. Why didn't you jump in when Rice's sister got her dander up?"

"Why would I, Martin? You did an exemplary job. Besides, it's only fair to share the fun."

Martin shook his head and gazed skyward. "Next time, feel free to do me a few less favors. I'm an expectant father. Stress could be harmful to the fetus. Do you think Rice's family is in danger, Pete?"

"The only thing I know is that, at this time, we can't provide protection for the family. That would never fly."

ELEVEN

Martin liked to do the driving, and Pete was happy with that arrangement. On the way to Nick Rice's neighborhood, Martin asked, "Have you formulated a plan for the rest of today?"

It was nearly seven o'clock, and the sun had set. Pete knew Martin was looking for a hint about when they would go home. He tried to be helpful. "Yeah, I don't think we should ring any doorbells after midnight. Surprisingly, it irritates some people. Then we get all those uncomplimentary letters in our personnel files."

"You know you should rethink your career, and consider seeking your fame on the comedy circuit," Martin said.

"Just checking to see if you're still awake. Let's split up and cover the homes closest to Rice's. Then we'll huddle and decide where to go from there. Worst case, we'll give up this effort by ten. I wonder if anyone who lives near Rice thinks he was being stalked or if he told any of them he thought so."

"Yeah, for sure. Wouldn't you talk to someone about it? He must have close enough friends to share that with. If he doesn't, what does that say about him?"

"Well, Martin, aside from meaning he wasn't being stalked and didn't think he was? The conversation about his sister could mean a hundred other things. If he suspected a stalker, it could mean he's the epitome of the private person. It could mean he knew who was stalking him and why, and was unwilling to give anyone a reason to look into it. I don't know. If we don't have any luck talking with the friends, family, and neighbors, the next step might be to dig into his life."

"I bet his family would appreciate that at a time like this."

"And how. That's why I'm trying to avoid it."

From the standpoint of expediting their investigation, the good news was that Heather said Nick's best friends were coworkers or lived in their neighborhood.

If the crime was the work of a stalker, Rice's neighbors and the neighbors of the vehicle owner seemed the most likely people to have detected that activity.

"What about the kid who usually drives the car that hit Rice? Why isn't he a priority?" Martin asked.

"He's a different sort of priority. If we find out someone was stalking Rice, I want to have a description of that person before we check out the owner's grandson. If the grandson was the driver, the fact that his fingerprints, DNA, you name it, are found in the car would be expected. He might be relying on that. If, however, the heat is on, he may take off. I'm doing everything I can think of to avoid giving him a head start."

The two investigators reached the street on which the Rice family lived. It was one block north of Wheelock Parkway and a bit east of the Gateway Trail. The homes were constructed in the sixties and seventies. Ranch-style homes with wood, vinyl, or cedar siding. Colors tended towards the natural, and ranged from white to dark brown. The lack of snow made it possible to see that the yards were nicely maintained. By all appearances, homeowners and/or renters were of one mind or compliant when it came to caring for their homes and yards.

Pete took Rice's side of the street, while Martin took the other side.

Both men hoped for a lucky break. A tidbit of information that would, minimally, narrow their search and, optimally, place them on the path to the LeSabre's driver. For now, they concentrated on the homes on Rice's block and across the street, as well as both sides of the street on the first block to the east and the west.

Pete found that most people in this middle-class neighborhood were home. All but one of them knew about the accident. They ranged in age from mid-thirties to elderly. The people with whom he spoke included two men that Heather described as Nick's "good friends." Neither of them, nor any of the other neighbors, felt that Nick seemed different in the recent past. In that time frame, he hadn't discussed any problems or concerns with them.

No one recalled seeing any suspicious activity in the neighborhood, including anyone they recognized or didn't recognize hanging around. However, one of Nick's friends said the woman who lived across the street from Nick and four houses down was the closest thing they had to a neighborhood lookout. "Her name is Sybil Wright," he said.

At Pete's request, he spelled the name. Then he added, "I think she's bored or lonely. Either that, or she's totally absorbed in the neighborhood. It could be her way of staying involved. She always knows what's going on around here. She knows if there's an unfamiliar car parked along our street for more than a day or two. She reports them to the police on a regular basis. I know that for sure, in one case, the car was either stolen or abandoned. This street might be quiet enough, you know, to make it a good dumping ground."

"Was she able to identify the person who left the car here?" Pete asked.

He was kidding, but the middle-aged man with a shaved head and goatee got up, saying, "Don't know. Hang on. I'll call her."

The man was already dialing the number by the time Pete could say, "Thanks, but my partner has either spoken with her or will shortly."

The only other currently valuable information he obtained was the names of a few more of Nick Rice's friends. He was anxious to hear what Martin uncovered, and if he'd discovered the neighbor-in-the-know.

TWELVE

Heading back to the unmarked car, Pete spotted Martin. He appeared deep in thought, as he made his way across the lawns, taking a shortcut to the house on the corner.

"Hold up," Pete called out and ran to catch up. Falling in stride with Martin, he asked, "Don't have all the answers yet?"

"Haven't asked all the questions." Martin smiled.

The couple who resided in the corner house looked close in age to Nick and Heather Rice. The man's receding hairline might skew at least half of that assessment. Both husband and wife carried enough spare pounds to make Martin look fit and trim.

Their son's willowy build accentuated the size of his parents. His hair was blond, with hints of red, and crept over the tops of his ears. Judging from his voice, he was prepubescent.

Moving from the front door, to the dining room, Pete noticed that the home was spotless. Even so, the hardwood floors and furniture showed signs of wear.

If curiosity is a sign of intelligence, the boy who lived here was a genius—or very nosy. He was tripping over his father's heels as his dad led the way to the dining room. His interest was explained, at least in part, when Ethan introduced himself as Alexis Rice's boyfriend.

Initially, the thirteen-year-old slowed the questioning by asking all kinds of seemingly inane questions. They included, "What do you mean, someone I haven't seen before? Like, if I saw him two or three times, does that count? Does it matter if I saw him here or a few blocks away? Do the days I saw him matter? I mean, are you talking weekdays, weekends, or does it have to be both?"

Ethan's saving grace came when he explained, "I have a morning paper route. I've seen a guy when I'm out delivering. Once he was in the front yard of the house next to ours. I only noticed him 'cause they get a paper, and he was just standing there. Afterwards, I never saw him on our street. The closest was on Iowa. I saw him once, I think on Edgerton, and once for sure on Wheelock Parkway."

Pete and Martin knew those streets. They were anywhere from a block away to within a quarter mile of the Rice home.

"When you saw him standing in the yard of the house next door, what direction was he facing?" Martin asked.

"West, I guess."

That was toward the Rice home.

"Where did he go after you saw him?" Martin asked.

"Don't know."

"About how old do you think this guy is?" Martin asked.

"Don't know. He wore a ski mask."

"Can you tell us what you do know about him?" Martin asked.

"He's taller than me—maybe like Dad. That's about all."

Martin knew that meant about his height—around five-ten. "How about his build?" he asked.

"Hard telling. He always wore a down parka. He looks fat. Could be the parka. Everybody looks fat in one. That's why I won't wear mine."

"You're a smart kid, Ethan," Pete said. "Lots of times there are clues a guy will pick up on. Clues that give a good idea about the person's size. Right? Could be things like the width of the ski mask or of the legs of the pants. Did you get any clues about this person?"

"I didn't pay attention to the shape of the ski mask, and he wasn't wearing skinny jeans. Besides, lots of fat old guys have bellies and skinny legs, like him." The kid moved his glance from Pete to Martin.

Martin's face reddened, and the kid's dad responded by poking him in the ribs with an elbow.

After the jab, the kid offered an unconvincing, "Sorry," and shrugged.

"We feel successful if we get you to wear a jacket at all, Ethan, much less anything resembling a hat," his mother sighed.

"What color was the jacket?" Pete asked.

"Navy blue."

"Much of this winter has been warm. When you saw this person, did it seem he was overdressed for the temperature? I'm referring to the down jacket and ski mask."

"It seems strange to see people wearing that stuff, unless the person's old and doesn't know any better. Seriously, who dresses that way? I figured he was homeless."

The look on the face of Ethan's mom clearly exhibited her displeasure with her son's mouth. Even so, she held her tongue.

"Setting aside your thoughts on fashion," Pete kidded, "did it seem this person had to be mighty hot wearing all those clothes?"

"Yeah. Like you said, it's been warm this year."

"Could you see this person's skin through the eyeholes of the ski mask?" Pete asked.

"Of course."

"What color was this person's skin?" Pete asked.

"White."

"You're sure about that?" Pete asked.

"Yup."

"Did this person look oriental?" Pete asked.

"No way." Ethan rolled his eyes.

"And you're saying that because... ?" Pete asked.

"Because of his eyes and his skin."

"And you saw this person before sunrise?" Pete asked.

"Yeah, for sure. In the winter, it's still dark when I deliver papers."

"Even though it was dark outside, you could tell the color of this person's skin?" Pete asked.

"Yeah. Even in the middle of the night, it isn't *that* dark around here. Especially if your house is on a corner."

"Based on the way this guy was dressed, he could be a she, right?" Pete asked.

Ethan shrugged and asked, "Would a lady wear a ski mask?"

"Did this person appear to be more interested in any particular part of the neighborhood?" Pete asked.

"Don't know. Didn't pay much attention. Had to deliver my papers, get home, and get ready for school."

"When did you last see him or her?" Pete asked.

"Not sure. It was a couple days ago or more. Maybe a week."

"When did you first see this person?" Pete asked.

"Two, maybe three weeks ago. After Christmas, I'm pretty sure."

"I'm impressed with your perceptiveness. I mean noticing all these things, Ethan," Pete said.

Thanking Ethan and his parents, Pete and Martin passed out business cards and returned to the unmarked.

"Wow, what were the chances of that happening?" Martin asked.

"Not good."

"The chances, or the information the kid provided?"

"The chances. Too bad he couldn't describe the person he saw."

"And too bad he didn't have the person's name and address. You aren't asking for much, are you?"

"Well, Martin, life is full of broken dreams."

"And you're a sorry excuse for a cop," Martin laughed.

"Tell me, Martin, do you know how to spell insubordination?"

That brought Martin up short. He never thought he'd hear Pete Culnane pull rank on anyone. Working frantically on a reply that would save his ass, Martin turned to Pete and said, "I didn't..." Seeing the broad smile on Pete's face, he knew he'd taken the bait, again.

Switching gears, Martin continued, "Before meeting that kid, I thought I had the discovery of the night. Then you joined me and forced that kid to spill his guts. The woman who lives in that house..."

Martin said, pointing to the house already identified by another neighbor as the residence of the neighborhood lookout.

"Let me guess," Pete said. "The woman who lives there saw someone hanging around the neighborhood in the last few weeks."

"How did you know?"

"I have ESPN."

"Huh? Oh, got it. Extra Sensory Perception—NOT!" Martin shook his head and laughed. "It's too late in the day to deal with this type of challenge. A murder investigation? Yes. A sick sense of humor? No way!"

"With a comeback like that, Martin, my feelings of insecurity are escalating."

"In your dreams, Pete, and only in your dreams."

"And those dreams would qualify as nightmares," Pete said, thinking Martin didn't know him as well as he'd suspected.

"Did this woman mention the times when she saw this person lurking around the neighborhood, or what they were wearing?" Pete asked.

"Her name is Sybil Wright. She wasn't sure if it was always the same person. Until the second time, she didn't pay that much attention to what they wore. I asked for a description of the person she also referred to as 'he.' It was pretty much a preview of what this kid said, only she thought the jacket was black, not navy. I think that's insignificant. In poor light, it's hard to distinguish between the two."

"Anyway," Martin continued, "she saw the person four times between five and six in the morning. I asked if she called the police and she said, and I quote, 'You're kidding, right? I don't think they'd consider it an emergency. I called 911 once about a problem with the house behind mine. They like to celebrate the Fourth of July as well as the third of July, and the fifth of July—all three late at night and with fireworks.'"

"She said she reports cars violating parking restrictions to the department's administrative number. According to her, 'Those people don't get all hot and bothered when someone calls about something that doesn't meet their definition of an emergency.' She doesn't believe calling the administrative number to report a person walking around the neighborhood early in the morning would accomplish anything. She said there was no telling if or when that person would do anything illegal. And she doesn't believe 'there's a chance in hell' the police would arrive while he was still in the vicinity."

"What's next on the agenda?" Martin asked.

THIRTEEN

ooks like I was whistling Dixie when I hoped Rice's neighbors might help us determine if he was being stalked," Pete said. "And if he was, I actually thought we might get at least a sketchy description of the stalker. Don't see any sense in delaying the questioning of Kevin Douglas any longer. Let's check him out. Maybe he'll pull out his down jacket and put it on for us."

"I'm concerned, Pete. Are the demands of the job causing you to lose touch with reality? Perhaps you should start exploring other options."

"Like going to tryout camp to see if the Twins will sign me? Do you think playing out in the elements at Target Field will wrinkle my skin?" Pete frowned and patted his cheek.

"Don't worry. The water boy doesn't get that much time in the sun. I bet you'll look real cute in a baseball jersey and cap. They're sure to turn Katie's head. You'll be on her radar and won't stand a chance."

Pete didn't need this mention of Katie to remind him of their plans for Saturday. He already knew that once again his timing seemed poor. If he canceled this weekend, it wouldn't be the first time—or the second. At this rate, would she tell him to take a hike? Was Katie capable of coping with this unpredictability? It seemed so, but wasn't optimism a characteristic of most failed marriages? The better he got to know her, the more he hoped she could deal with him and his lifestyle.

He didn't know how long this investigation would dictate his schedule. Thinking it wouldn't go past Friday seemed mighty optimistic. When should he call Katie to let her know about potential problems with their plans?

Martin parked in front of Kevin Douglas's home. The grandson of the Buick LeSabre's owner lived roughly a mile southwest of the accident scene, and not much further than that from Nick Rice's home. Did Kevin know Nick or his family? Giving Kevin the benefit of the doubt, if he was the person seen in the Rice neighborhood, was he trying to protect Rice's backside?

The home where Kevin lived with his mother was located in a hardworking middle-class neighborhood on St. Paul's East Side. Streetlights illuminated the area well enough for Pete and Martin to get a feel for the area. The pre-World War II homes were modest compared with those on the parkway and in Rice's neighborhood. Most were two stories and compact. Garages were detached or nonexistent.

Pete hoped to have answers to a few more questions after this next meeting.

It seemed the gods smiled down on either Martin Tierney or Kevin Douglas. Kevin wasn't home. Kevin's mother invited the two investigators to step inside, but that was the extent of her hospitality. She didn't invite them to have a seat. They spoke inside the front door.

Despite thin shoulders, the woman's stomach pushed out the front of her shirt. It didn't look like the type of bulge attributable to pregnancy. Her brown hair was thin and stringy, hanging in wisps almost to her shoulders. Her long-sleeved shirt and jeans looked rumpled.

The interior of her home had the charm and many of the amenities characteristic of the era. The baseboards were wide, dark oak. The home had plaster walls and built-in buffets and cupboards. A stained-glass window adorned the living room. This home had a personality that stood in stark contrast with much of modern construction.

Learning that the two investigators wanted to speak with Kevin—the usual driver of the LeSabre—Kevin's mother called his cell phone. He didn't answer. Her luck didn't improve when she called all of the phone numbers she had for his friends.

As she hung up the last time, she smiled apologetically and said, "Sorry. Want me to call you when he gets home—if he gets here before I leave for work?"

"Any idea when that'll be?" Pete asked.

Glancing at her watch, she said, "It's nine thirty. He's usually in before eleven on weeknights, because he has to get up for work the next day."

"What time does he leave for work?" Martin asked.

"Around six forty-five."

"Where does Kevin work?" Pete asked, checking to see if she'd provided the same answer her son gave the uniformed officers this morning.

"At the Cambridge Garden Center. Have you heard of it? It's four or five miles from here."

"Yes, I'm familiar with it, Ms. Douglas," Pete said.

"Murray, my last name is Murray. I wasn't married when Kevin was born. For that matter, I'm not married now, either." A "that's life" smile crossed her face.

Pete wondered if Kevin Douglas took all of this so nonchalantly.

"Did Kevin go to work this morning?" Martin asked.

"I assume so. He didn't say anything about not going."

"On the days he works, does he always start work at seven in the morning?" Martin asked.

"Yes, well, unless he's filling in for someone."

"Did you see him this morning?" Martin asked.

"No, I work the graveyard shift at a nursing home a few miles from here. We never see each other in the morning unless, of course, either Kevin or I have the day off."

"Has Kevin acted differently in the past few weeks or month? I mean, has he been more irritable, impatient, nervous? Anything like that?" Pete asked.

"No. Well, except that he's been pressuring me for information about his father. He gets testy when he thinks I'm withholding information."

"What kind of information?" Martin asked.

"He wants to know who his dad is."

"What did you tell him?" Pete asked.

"I told him the truth. I told him I don't know who it is." She looked embarrassed at the revelation.

"Did he accept that?" Pete asked.

"No. He wanted to know all of the possibilities. He demanded a list. I refused."

"Do you think he has some suspicions?" Pete asked.

"I don't know," she shrugged.

"If and when he identifies the man, what do you think Kevin will do?" Pete asked. He was considering the possibility that Kevin had discovered Nick Rice was his dad.

"Kevin hasn't had an easy life. He's gone without a lot of things other kids his age have. I wouldn't be surprised if he demanded money—a small part of the child support that was never paid."

"Is Kevin looking at any particular age group? Have you provided that type of information?" Pete asked.

"Funny you should ask. That's the one thing I was willing to tell him."

"And what did you tell him?" Pete asked.

"I told him his dad would be somewhere in the neighborhood of forty to forty-four."

"How did he react to that?" Pete asked.

"Like I'd just handed him a winning lottery ticket."

"Has Kevin modified his schedule during the past several weeks?" Pete asked.

"If he has, it wouldn't be a change I'd notice. My schedule versus his, you know what I mean?"

"I understand what you're saying. Do you rotate the days you work?" Pete asked.

"Yes, unfortunately. That's a mandatory part of the job. Not at all nursing homes, but it is at mine."

"How about Kevin? Does he work weekdays only?" Pete asked.

"He always works Monday through Friday. Why so many questions?"

"You see Kevin on the mornings you aren't working, don't you?" Pete asked.

"That would be unusual. By the time he gets up, I'm getting ready for bed or in bed trying to catch up on sleep. They say you'll sleep better if you stick with one schedule, you know."

"But you hear him moving around, getting ready for work," Pete said.

"Rarely."

"And you didn't see or hear him this morning?" Pete asked.

"No, I didn't because, like I told you, he left for work before I got home."

Pete and Martin left, after obtaining Kevin's cell and work phone numbers.

As Martin drove away from the Murray, or was it the Douglas home, Pete brought up the unthinkable, at least for him. "I think this is all we can reasonably accomplish today, Martin. Can you forgive me for cutting your day short?"

Martin's response was nonverbal. The streetlights allowed Pete to catch part of the reaction. Martin tilted his chin up and shook his head slowly from side to side.

Pete was confident Martin also rolled his eyes.

Driving home after dropping off Pete at headquarters, Martin thought about the matrix he'd developed last year. He was still trying to fine-tune—or better yet, perfect—it. The matrix was a system he used to track the suspects and all the potential motives, eliminating from both lists as the case progressed.

Pete supported this effort, but didn't seem to have any use for it. Perhaps that meant he was better at keeping things straight in his head. Martin hoped he could abandon it once he'd been an investigator as long as Pete.

His thoughts shifted to Michelle and their baby. He still couldn't believe it. After all the years of trying, they were actually going to have another baby. Why hadn't Michelle called about the ultrasound? Did she know if the baby was a girl or a boy? Was she waiting to see his face when she told him?

FOURTEEN

When Pete arrived at headquarters the next morning, Martin was already there. His head was propped up on his left hand. His gaze was fixated on his desk.

Martin wasn't lazy, but seeing him at headquarters this early surprised Pete. It also raised concerns about the results of Michelle's ultrasound. Did she have bad news? Was something wrong with the baby? Did Martin report in this early to escape?

As he approached, Pete noticed that Martin was working on his matrix. Was he that absorbed in this case? Still...

"How's it going?" he asked.

Martin looked up. His smile conveyed so much happiness that it was contagious. "Michelle had a party last night. She delayed it until I got home. She made devil's food cupcakes with pink frosting—to tell me the baby's a girl. I can't believe it, Pete. We're going to have a little girl. We're ecstatic! Michelle's painting and wallpapering the baby's room. She even wants to start shopping—for dresses, and who knows what else. You know how much I hate shopping. I told her I want to go along. I feel like a newlywed."

Martin beamed, and Pete was thrilled for his friend.

"I'd think after all that celebrating you'd have slept in this morning," Pete said. "You must have been up before dawn."

"Yeah, I was so hyper, I couldn't sleep. I lay awake most of the night, thinking and planning."

"Since you had all night, did you come up with a name? Something like Jackpot?"

"I'm not sure Michelle would go along with that."

"Well, if you insist on going conservative, Miraculous might be out, but there's always Grace."

"I was thinking more along the lines of Michelle, but I could run into some resistance there."

"Whose idea was it to name Marty after you?" Pete asked.

"Michelle's. I told her I preferred something like Jack, but she was insistent. I fought it tooth and nail. She won." Martin chuckled.

Pete patted Martin on the back. "I couldn't be happier for you. We'll continue the celebration at lunch. Let's head out."

Martin drove to the garden center where Kevin Douglas worked. It was after seven on a weekday. Kevin should be there.

Cambridge Garden Center was a familiar fixture for the residents of Maplewood, a suburb north of St. Paul.

While Martin drove, Pete called Kevin's cell. Waiting for him to answer, Pete wondered if Murray told her son that they were at his home last night. He hoped she left for work before Kevin got home. From what she said, she wouldn't return until after he left this morning.

If she didn't see him, did she leave a voicemail or written note? He hoped not. Advanced knowledge of the nature of his and Martin's questions could affect the answers. It could also give Douglas an opportunity to arrange an alibi. His mother already excluded herself from that role.

He wondered if Murray thought her son was guilty of something. More important, was he?

Pete reached Kevin Douglas's voicemail. He didn't leave a message. He knew Douglas's cell wouldn't identify him as Peter Culnane, nor as a part of the St. Paul Police Department.

Next he called Kevin's work number. When a woman answered, he asked for Kevin.

She said he was out, making deliveries. Her best estimate was that he'd return in a half-hour or an hour.

The woman said her job was working checkout and answering the phones, so she wasn't sure about Kevin's schedule. Yes, it was possible he'd be sent out on more deliveries. She said she had no way of knowing that.

Pete asked to be connected to Kevin's supervisor or a manager.

Valerie, the manager with whom Pete spoke next, was accommodating. She told Pete to ask for her when he arrived. She said that he and Martin could wait for Kevin in her office, and she would ensure that Kevin went there as soon as he returned.

In response to Pete's question, she said Kevin's responsibilities varied. They included watering and fertilizing plants, pulling weeds, removing dead foliage, and moving the inventory around the greenhouse. On a good day, as defined by her staff, he also tended the cash registers and made deliveries.

The two investigators walked into the garden center. It was primarily a greenhouse. Their nostrils were attacked by the cloying scents of the potted plants that crowded the interior. Ceiling-mounted sprinklers watered row upon row of wooden tables that displayed a variety of ferns and flowering plants.

Customers wandered around, inspecting the indoor plants and dish gardens.

Pete approached the cash register and waited for the clerk to finish with a customer. Then he identified himself and asked for Valerie.

A petite woman with a thick mane of blonde hair pulled into a ponytail arrived within a minute. She introduced herself and led the two investigators to her office. Once there, she asked if Kevin was in trouble.

Pete smiled and explained they had some questions regarding a car that belonged to Kevin's grandmother.

While they waited, Martin took advantage of the break in their schedule. He pulled the pages of his matrix from a suit-coat pocket and resumed his efforts. He wrote the names of the people with whom they'd spoken thus far in the left-hand column. Then he wrote possible motives along the top row. For now, those motives were broad categories.

A sudden realization brought him up short. If Rice's predicament was the result of an unintentional act, his matrix was of little to no value in this case. After pausing for a minute, closing his eyes, and rubbing his forehead, Martin continued writing.

Meanwhile, Pete called Regions and spoke with Nick Rice's doctor.

Rice remained on life support and in a medically induced coma. They were using EEGs to monitor brain swelling. No improvement. His thigh was shattered. Minimally, that surgery would be delayed a day or two.

Pete called Heather's cell phone. She was at the hospital. Nick's brother hadn't arrived. The trip from Fort McMurray to Edmonton, where Cory would board a plane for Minneapolis, was fraught with complications.

The company for which Cory worked arranged to fly him from Fort McMurray to Edmonton. Yesterday, a blizzard forced the closure of the Fort McMurray airport. Cory's departure from Fort McMurray was delayed until this morning. He made arrangements for an alternate flight out of Edmonton, and Heather expected him late this afternoon. As she rambled on about these arrangements, Pete heard the stress in her voice.

While he had her on the phone, he asked Heather about the friends named by a neighbor last evening. She said she knew them. She said they weren't as close to Nick as the people she listed. Even so, with her help and his cell, Pete found addresses and phone numbers for this second group of friends. Heather also knew where two of the three worked.

Next Pete called Rice's other coworker friend, Pat Steele. Voice-mail answered. He didn't leave a message.

Pete was putting his phone and notebook in their designated pockets when a young man appeared in the doorway of Valerie's office.

FIFTEEN

I'm Kevin Douglas," the man told Pete and Martin. "Understand you want to talk. What's up?"

Martin folded the pages of his matrix and returned them to his suit-coat pocket.

Pete instructed Kevin to come in, close the door, and have a seat. He motioned toward the chair across the table from Martin.

"Don't need to sit," Kevin said.

"Sit anyway," Pete said.

After Kevin sat down, Pete asked, "When's the last time you spoke with your mother?"

"A couple days ago. Why?"

"You haven't spoken with her at all yesterday or today?" Pete asked.

"No. Like I told you, I haven't talked to her in a couple days. If you don't believe me, ask her."

Pete studied the man. Per his driver's license, he was twenty-two. Judging from his appearance, the years had taken a toll. It looked like his favorite beverage was beer, and he had an unquenchable thirst. His brown hair looked shaggy. He was unshaven. His gray eyes conveyed suspicion. His clothes were clean, but bore signs of hard use.

"I run every day. You look like you do, too," Pete lied.

"Nope, don't have time."

"How do you spend your time?" Martin asked.

"I work, and I hang with my buddies."

"Where do you and your buddies hang?" Martin asked.

"Nowhere special. We move around. You know, spread the business, help the economy." Kevin's stare transformed into a smug smile.

"How about yesterday? What businesses did you assist yesterday?" Martin asked.

Douglas made a show of drawing upon his short-term memory bank. After what should have been enough time to balance his checkbook, he said, "I guess I was at Ben's house."

"And Ben's last name is?" Martin asked.

"Jackson."

"What's his phone number?" Martin asked.

"I don't remember."

"But you carry a cell phone. I'm confident you have him in your contacts list. Get it for me," Pete said.

Douglas reluctantly did as instructed.

"Many people your age use a cell phone in lieu of a watch. My guess is that you're one of them," Pete said.

"If you say so." Douglas sneered.

"What time did you arrive at Ben's?" Pete asked.

"I don't know. I was having fun. I wasn't worried about or interested in the time." In keeping with his performance thus far, Douglas didn't break eye contact with Pete during that recital.

"You have to get up to go to work. What time did you arrive home last night?" Pete asked.

"I don't know."

"But your mother was still there," Pete said.

"No, she wasn't."

"Do you use an alarm clock?" Pete asked.

Kevin Douglas looked at the table and paused before answering.

Pete wondered if he was considering whether they could check it out before he got home.

"Yeah," he said, finally, returning his gaze to Pete.

"What time did your alarm clock say it was?" Pete asked.

"Don't know. Didn't look."

"You know, we can always resort to a lie detector, don't you?" Martin asked.

"I also know the limitations of that technology." Again Douglas smiled, obviously pleased with himself.

"That's all for now," Pete said. "Make sure you don't leave town without checking with my partner or me first."

They each handed Kevin a business card.

Douglas piped up as the two investigators walked away. "Hey, before you leave, do I get to ask any questions?"

Both men turned and faced him. "Have at it," Martin said.

"I know you're here about that accident yesterday on Wheelock. I saw the remnants on my way to work. Can't believe someone stole my grandma's car. How's the injured guy doing? What did you say his name is?"

"What makes you think that's why we're here?" Pete asked.

"Get real. The bum used my grandma's car. She called. She doesn't want me to blame myself for it being stolen."

"Was the car stolen?" Pete asked.

"How else could anyone other than my grandma or me get it?"

"Thought you might know that," Pete said.

"No idea. Thought you might be able to tell me."

"Can't say. This is an active investigation," Martin said.

"Guess that means watch the news, huh?" Kevin shrugged.

Neither Pete nor Martin answered. They simply smiled, turned, and walked out of the office.

"That has to qualify as one of the best examples of an exercise in futility," Martin said as he and Pete walked to the unmarked car.

"I'd say we learned very little and a whole lot all at the same time," Pete said. "The words told us little. His demeanor spoke volumes."

"Yeah, you're right. Now that's one for the books."

Using his smart phone, Pete took a few pictures of Kevin Douglas's car, including one showing the license plate. You never could tell what might prove useful...

Both men sported smiles as they slid into the unmarked.

SIXTEEN

"W ho's next on your dance card?" Martin asked.

"Tell you in a minute." Pete pulled out his cell and dialed Pat Steele. The result was the same. Again, he left no message. He knew Steele wasn't due into Regisson until this afternoon. Regardless, it surprised him that he couldn't reach the man via his cell. Did Regisson prohibit its employees from talking on their cells while driving on company business? Even at a time like this, he endorsed that policy.

"Let's head back to Rice's neighborhood," Pete said. "I want to know if Sybil Wright recognizes Douglas's car... or a car that looks like his or his grandmother's."

"Due to her potential importance in this case," Martin said, "I've dubbed her 'the Wright woman.' That will make it impossible for me to forget her name."

"Speaking of names, what's happening with your matrix?"

Martin sighed. "So far, it's requiring a lot of time and providing zero answers. That's to be expected at this point. The fact there are so many names is just one reason why it's invaluable—at least for me. I'm hoping I'll be able to convince you of that by the time we wrap this one up. Time will tell. Well, time and an open mind. You qualify, don't you, Pete?"

"My mind is like the Twins' stadium, wide open. If I don't have enough time to see the value of your matrix beforehand, I promise to endorse it at my retirement party."

Martin shook his head. "If it takes until then to decide, it'll probably qualify as the world's most carefully contemplated endorsement.

We should submit it to Guinness. It could make it into a volume of *World Records*. Then we could combine that celebration with your retirement party. Wouldn't that be sweet? But, back to the investigation. Why doesn't Douglas just use his grandmother's car and get rid of his? Sounds like he's the only one who drives the LeSabre. It's a waste of money to insure both."

"His grandmother may be unwilling to relinquish control of her car. Kevin's role in getting her around might be temporary, or she could hope it is. Many elderly people continue holding onto their cars, because giving them up means the loss of independence and mobility. Both are hugely important to someone her age—heck, to people of all ages. Once done, it's often difficult or impossible to reverse. She may be fighting it tooth and nail. She may also feel she'd then have to pay for his insurance, since it's her car. A guy his age, even without any moving violations, has a significantly higher insurance rate than hers is likely to be. The actuarial charts don't help young males seeking car insurance. Sorry, I'll step down off my soapbox." Pete grinned.

"Actually, you're right on all counts. Just the same, if Kevin's the sole or primary driver, his grandmother should declare that."

"Yes, she should. Maybe she did. Lots of people don't."

"That can be a problem, if he's in an accident while driving her car."

"And many, many people ignore that, in hopes that, if an accident occurs, they can explain it away."

"And they succeed too often for the danger to serve as a deterrent." Martin frowned.

Pete snapped his fingers. "Bingo. That's the bottom line."

"Where's your money, Martin? Did Sybil see you drive up?" Pete asked, as Martin parked in front of Sybil Wright's home. She lived across the street and several houses east of the Rice family.

"Definitely, if she's doing her job as well as her neighbors claim."

Apparently the neighbors had her pegged. The Wright woman answered Pete's knock almost before his hand left the door.

"Come in. Please come in. So far this month, Martin, you're my number-one visitor. Who's your friend?"

Martin introduced Pete.

Sybil Wright appeared to be in her seventies. She had jet-black hair and a round face. Lipstick and blush suggested she was prepared, or hoping, for visitors.

Judging from her broad smile and bubbly personality, Sybil liked having company—or attention. That supported the neighbor's suggestion that she might watch activity in the neighborhood so closely because she was lonely.

"We're glad you're home," Pete said. "You were very helpful last night. We have a few more questions."

"Can I fix coffee? It will only take a minute. I have a Keurig. Are you familiar with them? They make coffee, tea, and hot chocolate one cup at a time. I have about a dozen flavors. Do you have a favorite?"

Sybil glowed. Was it the "visitors," or the fact she owned a Keurig? Was it the chance to extend the "visit?" Was it the thought of being an important part of the investigation?

Pete didn't have a clue. But it wasn't, thus far, relevant to the case. At her request, he and Martin followed Sybil into the kitchen. They sat around a sizable wooden table, adorned with a centerpiece of silk flowers.

Sybil read the list of flavors. While the coffee and tea brewed, she dished up a plate of cookies.

Utilizing the time, Pete learned she'd lived in this neighborhood for twenty-six years. She remembered the day the Rice family moved in, and she remembered the birth of each of their three children. She had fond memories of each child, especially Alexis.

Sybil told them about a meltdown at the Rice home. "Heather wanted another child. Nick responded by getting a vasectomy. I sided with both of them," she said. "Heather came over, crying. She couldn't believe Nick took such drastic steps to ensure she never got pregnant again. I told her he probably did it out of fear over an accidental pregnancy. I didn't think that was the reason. I just wanted to console her."

"What did you think?" Martin asked.

"My opinion was proven correct a few days later. I 'accidentally' ran into Nick in his yard." She smiled. "Estimates are that it now costs a quarter of a million to raise a child. For that reason, Nick believed that having another would require too much of a sacrifice for the five of them. He likes their lifestyle, and his toys. He doesn't want to change anything. Don't get me wrong. He's a wonderful person. He'd do anything for me. I love him like a son. He'll be okay, won't he?" Sybil brushed a tear way.

"His doctors are doing everything they can. That's all we know," Pete said.

"Anyway," Sybil continued, "Nick was unemployed for a long time. I think that's part of it. I think that made him more conservative with a buck. The important thing is, as long as he feels that way, I'm afraid there'd be hell to pay if Heather got pregnant."

Pete glanced at Martin, whose perspective on having another child couldn't be more different.

Martin didn't react, visibly, to the price tag Sybil and society placed on a child.

"I think it may have helped when I reminded Heather that it's now possible to reverse a vasectomy."

Sybil brought two mugs to the table and pushed the plate of cookies she previously deposited there to first Pete, then Martin.

Pete thanked her and put the smallest cookie on his plate.

True to form, or celebrating Michelle's pregnancy, Martin thanked Sybil and took two cookies. Another helping followed.

Pete showed Sybil the photo he took of Kevin Douglas's car and asked if she'd seen it in her neighborhood.

She looked at it long and hard, put her hand to her mouth, took in a deep breath and exhaled loudly.

SEVENTEEN

C ontinuing to concentrate on the photo, Sybil asked, "What kind of car is this?"

"It's a 2001 Ford Focus ZX3," Martin said.

"You know," Sybil said, "so many cars look the same these days. It isn't like it was when I was your age. Then, the cars manufactured by each company were so distinct. They didn't look like the cars made by any other company. I love seeing the classic cars when they have the car show or rally, or whatever it's called, at the state fairgrounds. There are always all sorts of cars from the fifties and sixties. Seeing them reminds me of the car I had back then. It was a 1958 Ford Fairlane. I loved that car! It was blue and white with a blue interior. It was the bee's knees. Sorry. You didn't come to hear about me." Sybil smiled apologetically. "Anyway, I may have seen this car. It isn't distinct in shape or color, so I can't be sure."

"Let me rephrase the question." Pete smiled. "Have you seen any small, black or dark-colored cars parked along this street? Cars that don't belong to neighbors? Cars you don't think you've seen before the last month or two?"

"Oh, that's much easier. Yes, I have."

"Tell us about the car or cars," Pete said.

Sybil leaned into the table, closing the distance between herself and the two investigators. She whispered, conspiratorially, "Early one morning, I saw a small, dark-colored car that didn't look familiar. I was surprised. It wasn't parked out front when I went to bed, but it was there when I woke up between five and six o'clock. After I put on my glasses, I realized that someone was sitting in the driver's seat.

I thought they were waiting for someone. I watched to see who they were picking up at that hour. No one got in the car. It sat there for at least fifteen minutes, then drove away." She added a hands-up shrug.

"Several days later," Sybil continued, "I again saw a car. It could have been the same car. Again it was about five or six in the morning. The car was parked in the same exact spot. The driver got out and crossed the street. He disappeared down the hill that runs behind the houses on that side of the street. The drop-off behind those houses gives the people who live in them a wonderful view of downtown St. Paul. At least it does in the winter. Heavens," she laughed, "I sound like a real estate agent."

"The time you saw the person get out of the car came after the time the person stayed in the car?" Pete asked, jotting down notes.

"Yes, I'm sure. After the first time, I was surprised to see him get out of the car. I thought he'd just sit there, again, and eventually leave."

"Can you be specific about where this car was parked?" Pete asked.

"Yes, on this side of the street and about halfway between my house and the one next door—the one to the west."

"Could you tell if the person sitting in this car was a man or a woman?" Martin asked.

"No. I think it was the same person both times, but I'm not positive. I thought the person who got out of the car was a man, but I'm not positive about that, either. It's so hard to know. He or she wore a very bulky hooded jacket. The kind usually worn by men, not women. I never saw the face. All I saw was the person's back. The hood was up, so I didn't see the hair."

"What color was the jacket?" Pete asked.

"It was a dark color. When I spoke with Martin last evening, I was sure it was black. I thought about it after you left, Martin." Sybil smiled at him. "It could have been something like navy or a dark plum color. It's so hard telling. The bulbs they now put in streetlights don't provide as much light as the old ones. It's harder to see things, especially colors."

"Despite the limitations due to the lighting, did you notice any rust on the car?" Pete asked.

"I didn't notice rust, but that doesn't mean anything. I can't really say if there was or wasn't any."

"Have you seen an unfamiliar rust-eaten black car hanging around the area?" Pete asked. He was describing the 1991 Buick LeSabre.

"Do you mean a little rust or a lot of rust?"

"A significant amount of rust on the side panels of a medium-sized black car. It would be a larger car than the car in the picture I showed you," Pete said.

"No, I haven't seen a car like that. Is that the car that hit poor Nick?"

"One like it," Pete said.

"Then you think he was being stalked? Oh, my gosh, that's terrible!"

"You said you never saw that car, Sybil. We don't know that Nick was being stalked. At this point, we're gathering information and getting answers," Pete said.

"Let's go back to the car or cars you saw early two different mornings," Martin said. "Do you remember which days you saw the car or cars?"

"I can't give you the exact dates or days of the week. I know that both times it was a weekday, and I know that neither time was this week. I believe the two times were about a week apart. I'm afraid I can't be more specific than that. Sorry, I'd have paid more attention had I known it was important."

"I understand," Martin said. "Do any of your neighbors have a car like the one you're talking about?"

"Yes, in fact, let's look out the window. It may be there now."

Pete and Martin followed Sybil to the picture window in her living room.

After looking west, she turned back to them and shrugged. "No, wouldn't you know it. It's gone."

"Which house were you looking at?" Pete asked.

"The dark-brown one on the other side of the street." Sybil pointed. "The one with the cedar shakes."

"Is there usually someone there at this time of day?" Martin asked.

Sybil looked at a watch that had the tiniest face Pete had ever seen, and shook her head. "It's no wonder the car isn't there. The kids are still at school."

"Is there a chance that the car you saw belongs to the people who live in that house? Might they have parked where you saw it? Could they have been sitting there so long, because they were texting or talking on the phone?" Martin asked.

"If they didn't want to park in their driveway, and they always do, there's plenty of space closer to their house. Why would they park way back here?"

"Did you notice anyone lurking around your neighborhood in addition to the two times you saw someone in a car?" Pete asked.

"Yes, remember, Martin? Yesterday I mentioned four times. Two of those times were when I saw the person in the car. The two other times, I saw the person, but not the car. Once the person was walking, the other time they were running. Each time I saw this person, it was between five and six in the morning. Each time the person wore a dark-colored hooded jacket. It always seemed to be a man, but it may have been a woman. I can't even guarantee," Sybil shrugged, "it was the same person all four times."

"When were the two times you saw the person outside of the car, relative to the two times you saw someone in a car?" Pete asked.

"Both were after the times in the car. One was last week. The other time was two days ago, on Monday."

"No one is looking for a guarantee, Sybil." Pete smiled. "If you were to give me your best guess, was the person you saw walking and running the same person who got out of the car?"

"I think so. The clothing was either the same or very similar."

"The walker and runner, what direction or directions were they headed?" Pete asked.

"East, both times."

"Did you watch them until they disappeared from view?" Pete asked.

"Yes. They both continued east, until I could no longer see them."

"Did you mention these observations to anyone?" Pete asked.

"I told my son. He said I have a vivid imagination and should get a hobby. I have two hobbies. I knit or crochet all the time. When I told him that, he said I should spend more time looking at what I'm knitting and crocheting, and less time spying on my neighbors. After thinking about it, I decided he might be right. Anyway, I decided to do a better job of keeping my mouth shut."

"From what I've heard, you provide a service to your neighbors. You may want to take your son's advice with a grain of salt," Pete said.

"Really?" Sybil's smile was infectious.

EIGHTEEN

For the third time that day, Pete called Rice's coworker, Pat Steele. It wasn't yet noon. Pete was, if anything, tenacious. This time, he left a message, explaining who he was and asking Steele to call ASAP.

Since they were in the neighborhood, he and Martin returned to the paperboy's home.

Ethan's mother didn't recall seeing Kevin Douglas's black Ford Focus or his grandmother's black LeSabre in her neighborhood.

While Martin drove toward headquarters, Pete called the list of Nick Rice's other friends. This was the list he'd compiled, courtesy of Rice's neighbor. He struck out with the home phone numbers, but connected with one of the three at his work location. Pete arranged a one o'clock meeting with that man, Chris Becker.

He tried Pat Steele's number again. He and Martin had two hours before the meeting with Becker and, in a roundabout sort of way, the trip to Regisson Medical was between headquarters and Becker's office.

Pete smiled when Steele answered.

Steele was on his way to the office and said he'd intended to return Pete's call as soon as he arrived. He said he'd be at Regisson in less time than it would take for Pete and Martin to get there.

Pat Steele met the two investigators at the reception desk. After expediting their trip through security, he led them to his office. He was nearly Pete's height, and built like a trim football player. He had straight blue-black hair, bright blue eyes, and a warm smile.

Steele expected to hear from the cops. He heard about Rice from Brian Traverse, and on the news.

"I can't believe it! How's Nick doing? I don't want to bother Heather."

Pete explained they knew little more than that he was in critical condition. He asked about Nick's demeanor in the last few weeks.

Steele said Nick seemed more anxious, tense, edgy, and he was getting worse. When he asked about it, Nick said it was nothing in particular and everything in general. Steele didn't accept that.

"Nick and I became good friends right after he started working here. That was three years ago. I cornered him after he told Brian and me that his sister had a problem with a stalker. I came right out and asked him if the problem was his, not his sister's. He fumbled for an answer and couldn't look me in the eye. I knew I was right. I tried to get him to admit it. I couldn't understand the secrecy. I told him I wouldn't tell anyone. I said I just wanted to help. He got angry. I changed the subject. I hoped he'd bring it up, when he was ready. Guess he didn't have the chance. Poor Nick. I wish I could have helped him. I hope he pulls through and not just for his sake. I feel so bad for Heather and the kids."

"Any idea why Nick refused to discuss his concerns or fears?" Pete asked.

"I don't know. Believe me, I thought about it a lot, even before this happened. Nick is usually an open book."

"Are you aware of Nick having any problems or altercations?" Martin asked.

Steele thought long and hard before saying, "It's a stretch. I hesitate to mention it, because Nick wasn't himself that night."

"We'll keep that in mind. Tell us about it," Martin said.

"The only thing I can think of is a problem he had with a waiter at the restaurant where Regisson Medical had our holiday party. Regisson paid for a chauffeur to drive all of us home. Nick drank far more than I've ever seen him drink. I figured the free drinks and ride home were the reason. Now I'm not so sure. My wife and I shared a table with Nick, Heather, and two other couples. Our waiter was young and overly solicitous. Nick thought he was hitting on Heather. I have to admit, it looked that way to me, too. It seemed like Heather was eating it up and egging the waiter on. Nick bent over and whispered something to her. She laughed, and he exploded." Steele frowned.

"I never saw Nick act that way. When the waiter returned with a tray of drinks and continued hitting on Heather, Nick jumped up. The tray went flying, and Nick reamed the guy out. The manager rushed over. Nick told the manager he'd never again set foot in Locker's." Steele bit his lip and shook his head.

"Seriously, it was the first time I ever saw Nick like that. He's usually so affable. The manager was very apologetic. He offered to get us a different waiter and give Nick a gift card. Nick told him that would be of little use. Said he'd never return, and he would never recommend the place to anyone. Nick and Heather left. I didn't see the waiter again that night. Who knows, maybe Nick got the guy fired."

"When was that party?" Martin asked.

"Due to scheduling problems, the party was delayed until January seventh."

"How would the waiter know Nick's name?" Martin asked.

"I'm sure I said his first name in front of the waiter at least once. I don't know how he'd get Nick's last name. Guess he could have asked someone. Still, it seems over the top to think that guy went after Nick. I guess you can never tell."

"This party was at Locker's?" Pete asked.

"Yes. The one in White Bear Lake."

"Do you know the waiter's name? Did he introduce himself?" Pete asked.

"He may have introduced himself, but I don't remember his name. Sorry."

"No problem. I'm sure the manager will remember the incident and the waiter," Pete said.

"That didn't sound like the Nick Rice we've heard about prior to this," Martin commented as he and Pete walked back to the unmarked.

"I agree. Would you be jealous if someone was flattering Michelle and she flirted with him?"

"No. I'm not that insecure, and I know Michelle. Rice is a good-looking guy, and he has a good job. What would make him that insecure, Pete?"

"A midlife crisis? Heather was trying to make him jealous?"

"Well, Pete, it could be her regular way of interacting with men."

"Wouldn't the CEO of a corporation hear about a meltdown at the holiday party?"

"I assume so."

"Yesterday, the CEO sang Rice's praises. He didn't utter a single negative thing about Rice. Steele is the first and only Regisson employee to mention it. Why is that?"

"Maybe the corporate culture dictates they say only good things about the dead and dying. Or, maybe all of their mothers drilled it into them."

NINETEEN

Chris Becker's office was the next stop. He was a CPA with his own accounting firm in Stillwater.

One of Minnesota's oldest towns, Stillwater was incorporated in 1854—on the same day as St. Paul, and more than a decade ahead of Minneapolis. Abundant lumber and a high level of river traffic were the drawing cards for the early settlers. Antique shops, new and used bookstores, restaurants, historic sites, and the scenic St. Croix River continued to attract visitors to this quaint river town.

Thankfully Pete and Martin didn't make the trip during rush hour. Going from Stillwater to St. Paul in the morning, and the reverse trip in the evening, made rush hour between Minneapolis and St. Paul look like a Sunday School picnic.

The two cops drove through downtown Stillwater on their way to Becker's office. En route, they passed Darn Knit Anyway.

"Hey, Katie talks about that place," Pete said, noticing the sign and pointing at the well-preserved brick building. "She takes her grandmother there. Her grandmother taught her to knit when she was only about ten."

"Does Katie bring her knitting along on your dates, in an effort to avoid boredom during the lapses in conversation?"

"She did, but stopped a week or two ago." Pete laughed.

"Michelle loves Stillwater. In addition to the shopping, she likes eating on one of the patios and watching the river traffic."

"I agree with your wife. Dad and Mom brought us here when I was a little kid. Loved it then, love it now. Don't make it back as often as I'd like."

Becker's office was located high on the hill, on the first floor of a century-old home. It overlooked downtown Stillwater, the lift bridge that was creating such a stir, and the St. Croix River. On a slow day, which for an accountant had to be sometime after April, the view from Becker's desk could entertain the average guy for hours.

Chris Becker was built like a boxer. His triceps and biceps tested the stitching on his Oxford cloth shirt. He had medium brown hair, and a goatee that was several shades darker.

The decor inside this stately old house preserved the original style. Wide oak baseboards matched the trim that ran along the ceiling. The walls were covered with wallpaper that displayed large sprays of flowers. The curtains were lace. The furniture looked antique. It seemed like curious décor for a man's office.

Pete commented that it was nice to see that Becker preserved the home, rather than gutting it and starting over.

"It belonged to my grandparents," Becker said. "I couldn't bear to change it. Guess I've created a monument to them." He chuckled.

Pete and Martin sat across the desk from Becker and ran through the usual list of questions. They hoped for a few answers that would steer them in a new and fruitful direction.

They weren't totally disappointed.

"Right after the first of the year," Becker said, "Nick and I were on our way to a Timberwolves game. They've finally gotten the fire. For the first time since Garnett was traded, we may actually have a team. I'm sure you know how traffic is whenever there's a sporting event downtown. It doesn't matter if it's the Wild playing in St. Paul, or the Timberwolves, Twins, or Vikings in Minneapolis. Rush hour is bad enough without the throngs drawn to the games. On game night, everyone is making a mad dash to get to the game on time or escape that frenzy. Life would be easier for everyone concerned if the weekday games started a half-hour later. Sorry, I digress."

"Nick and I were in downtown Minneapolis, near the Target Center, when this moron took a right turn on red and came within a hair of hitting a pedestrian. Nick caught up with him at the next light. He jumped out of the car, ran up to the guy, and started screaming at him. The light changed and Nick ran back, jumped in, and kept driving. He continued ranting. The jerk pulled over and followed us all the way into the parking ramp. As soon as Nick got out of the car, the bastard started swinging at him. Nick punched him in the gut so hard, the guy bent over and couldn't stop coughing."

"What did you do then?" Martin asked.

"We went to the game." Becker reddened.

"You know, it's a bad idea to accost anyone in this day and age," Pete said. "People get shot for those sorts of things—and for much less."

"Yeah, I know. I never would have done it. I told Nick that, too. He said he did it on the spur of the moment, because the woman in the crosswalk was so close to being hit. He said she might have been killed."

"Still seems like an overreaction," Martin said.

"Yes, but it made more sense when Nick added, 'Did you see the woman he almost hit? She could have been Heather's twin.'"

Becker's description of the man Nick punched fit about a half-million men living in the Twin Cities area. And, of course, Becker didn't know if he was local. The man could have driven a significant distance into downtown Minneapolis for the game. He might have been there for a variety of other reasons. He might have flown into the Twin Cities on business. He could live anywhere.

Becker said he didn't pay any attention to the man's car or the license plate. He was too busy watching the woman and his friend.

Pete shook his head all the way back to the car. "I can't believe anyone would be so unthinking, or stupid, in this day and age. If that was the triggering event, there's a distinct possibility that Rice will pay with his life. Finding the guy he punched could be the all-time challenge of my career. Thankfully, Becker knew the Wolves played the Grizzlies that night. Now we can determine the date. Maybe someone saw the confrontation, wrote down the license plate number, and registered a complaint with the Minneapolis PD. Wouldn't that be sweet?"

"Yup, and don't forget to start working on next year's wish list for Santa."

While Martin drove, Pete used the browser on his cell to look up the date of the Timberwolves-Grizzlies game. Despite the frequent intrusions into his life initiated by this device, Pete loved the information it delivered when he used the web browser.

Once he had the date—January 4—he called a buddy with the Minneapolis PD. Pete wanted to know of any reports of an incident in the vicinity of the Target Center, between five and eight that evening. It felt like it took an eternity before he received the negative response.

Martin was right. He'd have to put away his letter to Santa—at least until after the Easter Bunny dropped off his basket, or they got a break in this case, whichever came first.

TWENTY

Back at headquarters, Pete and Martin took turns arranging the meetings with Nick Rice's remaining friends—the ones mentioned by a neighbor.

That accomplished, Martin said, "So, we have time and it's almost two. How about breaking for lunch?"

"If we do, will we be broken men?"

"Huh? Oh, never mind." Martin rolled his eyes. The motion was so pronounced, his head followed the same path.

Food summoned Martin throughout the day. If it was deep fried, it was a sure bet he loved it.

When he hit thirty, Pete trained himself to stick with choices that had less fat and more nutrition. He disciplined himself to prioritize the way he looked over the fleeting pleasure provided by food. Unlike Martin, he found the rewards outweighed the sacrifices. Life sometimes intervened, but he tried to minimize the exceptions.

Pete often avoided cooking, by eating his biggest meal at lunch. Like many, he found cooking for one unappealing.

Except on rare occasions, regardless of when Martin arrived home, his wife prepared his dinner. Her motivation may have been to ensure Martin followed the diets she had him on perpetually. She could oversee dinner, so Martin made the most of lunch—by way of every possible meaning assigned to that term.

Pete picked up the check, in honor of Martin's daughter-in-process.

After lunch, they chased from St. Paul to Arden Hills and Roseville, meeting with the remaining friends. En route, Pete forced himself to entertain the possibility it was a hit-and-run, not an intentional attack. If it was, he hoped the driver's conscience and the TV announcements soon sparked a confession—or a call from an informant.

Time would tell if lunch was the highlight of the afternoon.

During the next two meetings, Pete and Martin planned to look for other facets of Nick Rice's personality, contradictory information about Nick, and additional indications that Nick became unusually argumentative in the past two to three weeks. Both the Regisson Medical holiday party and the Timberwolves game Rice attended occurred during that time frame.

The first friend, Roger Grant, looked twenty years older than Rice and his other friends. His hair was salt-and-pepper and combed back on the top and sides. Pete was tempted to check to see if he had a ducktail. Compared to Nick and his other friends, this man looked out of shape. Pete wondered if the added years explained it.

Grant said he hadn't seen Rice in more than three weeks.

Even so, the two investigators ran through the drill.

"I've never seen him in a confrontation or acting aggressively," Grant said. "That just isn't Nick. He never lets anything bother him. He's kept me out of a few fights. He claims I have a short fuse," Grant smiled, holding his thumb and index finger an inch apart.

"Does Nick gamble or have any financial problems?" Pete asked.

"No, I'm certain Nick doesn't have any financial problems or a gambling addiction. He's very conservative when it comes to the way he handles money. Other than his home, if he can't pay cash for something, he doesn't buy it."

When Pete moved from money to love as the potential motive, Grant said, "I'm confident neither Nick nor Heather are having or have had another romantic interest. Have you ever seen the two of them together?" he asked, before realizing the absurdity of the question.

"I'm astounded that something like this could happen to a guy like Nick," Grant insisted.

After Grant spent five minutes expanding upon that, Pete and Martin wondered if he was a bit too emphatic. Martin added Roger Grant to his matrix, and Pete handled it in his usual manner—a note in his spiral notepad.

The second friend, Jeff Mower, had a shaved head and a stud in his left earlobe. The sleeves of his shirt were rolled up past the elbows. Pete thought he might be attempting to withstand the uncomfortably warm temperature in his office at the Minnesota State Lottery.

The two investigators asked about unusual actions over the last month.

Mower saw Nick after the first of the year. He, too, was hard-pressed to name any likely enemies, even those as distant as the waiter and the man Nick confronted before the Timberwolves game.

"Have you noticed any changes in his personality over the last month or six weeks?" Martin asked.

"Nick's been jittery, restless, incapable of relaxing. For instance, the last time I saw him, he kept checking over his shoulder. It was like he anticipated running into someone he didn't want to see. Judging from the look in his eyes, he almost seemed scared. You'd have thought I was a woman, and he expected Heather to walk in on us."

"Where were you when this happened?" Martin asked.

"At the Wild hockey game at the Excel. He was making me a little crazy. He tried to cancel at the last minute. I couldn't find anyone else on such short notice. I pretty much forced him to go. He was such a wreck. Neither of us enjoyed the game, even though the Wild won."

"What was the date of that game?" Martin asked.

"January tenth."

"Did you ask him why he was so nervous?" Pete asked.

"Of course. He claimed it was the emotional baggage tied to cutbacks at Regisson Medical. I don't know much about Regisson, so I left it at that."

"You mentioned that at the Wild game, Nick acted almost like he feared Heather finding him with another woman..."

"Yeah," Mower interrupted Pete. "That was just what came to mind. No, Nick doesn't have a girlfriend!"

"You know that for a fact?" Pete asked.

"I'm positive. He doesn't show any of the signs."

"How about Heather?" Pete asked. "Is she having or has she had an affair?"

"All I can say is, I wouldn't believe it if anyone told me she did."

On the way to headquarters, Pete asked Martin, "Did any of the employees or anything you saw lead you to believe that cutbacks were underway at Regisson?"

"Not a chance. Quite the opposite."

"Me, too. To the extent we can rely on what we're hearing, here's Rice's recent past. He was antagonistic on January fourth and again on the seventh. On the tenth he was a nervous wreck. Sound to you like he might have thought he was being stalked, Martin?"

"Sounds reasonable. If I was being stalked, I might make that transition. I might be angry when I realized it was happening. If I discovered I couldn't stop it, fear would be a reasonable reaction. But I think I'd make a concerted effort to bring a screeching halt to the situation."

"How would you do that?"

"I'd bring the problem to your attention, of course." Martin grinned.

"That would be a brilliant move on your part, Martin, but Nick Rice was unaware of my extraordinary talents. He didn't know he should contact me. If you were in his shoes, what would you do?"

"I'd be careful, watch my backside, and hope the person dug him or herself into a hole."

"And for all we know, that's exactly what Rice was doing."

"True. Sounds like you're convinced he was being stalked, Pete."

"Don't know for sure. His behavior makes it plausible. I hope his brother isn't delayed, again. I'm hoping he can answer that question. I'm also anxious to get his take on Nick's positive and negative sides. What do you think, Martin? Will a guy share the negative side of a brother at a time like this?"

"It would take a lot for me to do that. How about you?"

"You're right, Martin. I think the circumstances would have to be pretty extreme. They are."

TWENTY-ONE

Pete called a friend in the Traffic and Accident Division. He wanted an estimate of the LeSabre's speed when it hit the curb. It might give him a feel for the driver's frame of mind at the time of the crash.

He learned that unofficial and preliminary estimates had the car traveling between fifty and sixty miles per hour when it hit the curb. When the blown front tires came in contact with the median, they dug in and skidded across the surface. The skid continued for several feet before the LeSabre struck Rice, plowing him into the tree. The estimated speed, at the time Rice was hit, was between ten and twenty miles per hour.

Obviously, that was enough to kill someone, especially when the impact smashed the victim's head into a tree, causing a traumatic brain injury.

Pete's efforts to maintain objectivity were jolted when they ran smack into the next revelation. The rubber left on the pavement near the intersection where the crash occurred matched the LeSabre's tires. Those tires were eight years old. The age and condition of the tires eliminate most other cars from consideration.

Valuable information, but Pete resolved to keep it from dictating his perspective. There were too many other variables to consider, and there were volumes of documented cases where someone intended to step on the brake and floored the gas pedal.

He thought about some of the explanations. Did the driver evaluate the parkway prior to the event, looking for the best location? If not, what were the chances of it happening at the intersection providing the most obstructed view for the residents on the south side of the parkway?

If it was planned, did the driver intend to hit Rice as he crossed the street? Worse yet, from the standpoint of treachery, did it unfold without wavering from the plan?

Did Rice attempt to dodge the LeSabre? Did the driver react to Rice's maneuver, going up and over the curb in a desperate attempt to either hit or miss him?

Pete was reminded of another possibility. Rice wore all dark clothing, and it was dark at the time of the incident. Streetlights provided some illumination. Enough for the driver to see Rice? That depended on the driver. Sybil Wright demonstrated the problems older adults have with the current lighting. Did the driver see Rice at the last second, and go over the curb attempting to avoid him?

The extinguished headlights provided no absolute answers. The driver may have left them off to avoid detection by Rice. On the other hand, streetlights illuminated city streets well enough to permit driving without headlights. It was common to see drivers who failed to turn them on after sunset, when the level of lighting was similar to the level yesterday morning. Over the years, he'd pulled over and nudged more than one driver who got in their car after dark and failed to turn on their lights. How unusual was that? Did it happen morning and evening?

All of this back and forth between premeditated and accidental made Pete feel befuddled.

The final note from Pete's friend was that the steering wheel and door handles had been wiped clean. Did that indicate intent, relative to theft of the LeSabre, or was the driver trying to cover up a more serious crime?

Pete's thoughts switched to the lingering signs that an accident occurred on Wheelock Parkway. Bark was stripped from the tree against which Rice was pinned. There were marks where the blown tires dug into and scarred the median. Both reminded passersby of the events of yesterday morning.

He hoped the Rice family didn't travel this route on their way to school, work, or other activities. Thankfully, the accident scene wasn't along the path from their home to Regions Hospital.

TWENTY-TWO

It was six p.m. The sun disappeared an hour ago. The two investigators hadn't heard from Nick's brother or any member of the Rice family. They weren't surprised. Neither assumed they'd be the family's top priority.

For them, however, speaking with Nick's brother Cory was the top priority. Had he arrived in the Twin Cities?

They decided to go to Regions Hospital. When circumstances permitted, they would reiterate the importance of speaking with Cory at the earliest opportunity.

The ICU buzzed with activity this evening. Nurses scurried from room to room. Pete wondered if it had anything to do with the hour.

Things were also in motion near Nick Rice's room. His sister and children arrived. All four looked more composed, but no happier, than the last time the two investigators saw them.

Pete wondered about Rice's status. Was he still on life support? He knew Rice was still alive. Headquarters would have been notified if he died, and headquarters would have immediately notified Martin and him. They would also have heard if he regained consciousness.

He decided to take advantage of the down time to think about the investigation—what they'd accomplished thus far, and what they may have overlooked. Pete did this each night on his way home. Unless he passed out when his head hit the pillow, he invariably also contemplated it for a while as he lay in bed.

The items on their to-do list could be dictated and prioritized by the things they learned from Cory. They had to talk with his sister and some of Rice's neighbors again. So far, they had only shown Sybil

Wright and the paperboy's mother the photo of Kevin Douglas's car. They had to find out about the waiter who infuriated Rice at Locker's Bar and Grill. Did he still work there? If not, Pete wanted to talk to some of the other employees. Either way, he wanted to speak with the waiter. If Cory Rice didn't create a different priority, a visit to Locker's might be the next item on their agenda.

As he turned to discuss that with Martin, Pete heard the muffled ding of the elevator bell. He turned back and watched two men emerge. Either might have been Cory Rice, but neither man bore a resemblance to Nick or Sarah.

The younger one looked a few years older than Nick. He had brown hair that was gray at the temples. He wore a suit and tie.

The second, older man was more rotund. His eyebrows were significantly thicker than the hair on his head. He wore large, black-framed glasses with thick lenses.

The two men spoke as they exited the elevator, increasing the likelihood they were together. Talking to a stranger in an elevator was a rare occurrence, even in Minnesota.

Pete watched, wondering if they were the exception that proved the rule. When the older man followed the younger one into Nick's room, Pete's mind raced. Who would Cory bring along at a time like this? Had Nick's condition changed?

Cory scrambled to reach the Twin Cities. Did this man assist with those efforts? Was he the specialist Heather mentioned consulting for a second opinion?

Pete decided there were at least 100,000 possibilities. His thoughts were interrupted.

The two men from the elevator stepped into the hallway with Heather Rice. The older man spoke, while Heather listened with her eyes closed, nodding from time to time.

In less than a minute, she collapsed against the second man. He embraced her tightly and stroked her back. They stood that way a couple of minutes, while the older man continued his monologue.

When he finished talking, he reached for Heather and squeezed her arm.

She nodded and took a step back from the man who'd held her. After patting her eyes with a tissue, she pasted an expression that was a few degrees less distraught on her face.

The man who'd held her kissed her cheek, and put an arm around her shoulder. He kept it there as they re-entered Nick's room.

The second man followed. His body language suggested a personal link to Rice or his family.

Several minutes later, people began departing Nick's room. Sarah and the three Rice children were the first to leave. All were crying. Rice's daughter sobbed.

Sarah didn't acknowledge Pete. Her head and the heads of the three children hung low as they shuffled to the elevator. They moved as a tight little mass, seemingly neither knowing nor caring what was in their path.

TWENTY-THREE

The two men who'd spoken with Heather in the hallway exited Rice's hospital room and approached Pete and Martin.

"Commander Culnane, Sergeant Tierney?" the younger man, the one who'd held Heather, asked.

The two investigators nodded, and both extended a hand.

"My name is Cory Rice. I'm Nicky's brother. This is Dr. Henry Kittson. He's a buddy of mine. He came to consult with, guess I should say to counsel, Heather. Dr. Kittson had to wait for a member of the family before Nicky's doctor could speak with him. We were returning from that meeting when we got off the elevator and passed you. Sorry I ignored you. I had, have, a lot on my mind."

Cory went to the nurses' station and asked to use a conference room.

The nurse gave them directions to a room outside the ICU.

After they reached that location and arranged four chairs in a circle, Cory continued. "Hank drove down from Duluth and picked me up at the airport. Hank, please explain what Nicky's doctor said. I can't talk about it," he added, rubbing a hand through his hair.

"Please, stop me if this is repetitive or more than you care to hear," Kittson said. "Nick sustained an SAH, a subarachnoid hemorrhage. The blow to the back of his head knocked him unconscious and caused significant swelling of his brain. He's in a medically induced coma to protect his brain. His body has to absorb the blood. This problem cannot be addressed surgically. Nick's status is being monitored, using EEGs and blood work. So far, there's no significant change. Best case scenario, he could be weaned from the coma in another day or two. Once Nick is stabilized, he'll require a surgical repair to his shattered femur."

"Heather believes the fact Nick is alive is a miracle," Cory said. "She refuses to believe he'll do anything but fully recover, despite the odds. Do you believe in miracles?" he asked, looking at Pete and Martin.

"Absolutely. I see them every day," Pete said.

Cory nodded. "Heather wanted to hear about Nicky's condition and possible outcomes in layman's terms," he explained. "The doctors treating Nicky are excellent, but it means more coming from someone who has a personal connection with our family."

Turning from Pete to Kittson, Cory said, "Thanks, Hank—for everything. They have some questions for me. I don't want to keep you waiting. I'll see you later."

Kittson asked if he could wait somewhere, and give Cory a ride to Heather's.

Cory thanked him and said, "I need some time alone—time to work through things. Dismissing the other man, he added, "I'll see you tomorrow afternoon." Then he stood and hugged Kittson.

Kittson walked away, reluctantly.

When Cory sat down, Pete saw that his eyes were moist. He wondered if Cory had put on a front for his brother's family.

"Nicky's a wonderful guy, and I know him down to his very soul," Cory said. "Usually the younger brother looks up to his big brother. I guess he did as a young kid, but I've looked up to him for years. He's always there for me. And what did I do? I let him down when he needed me most. I asked him to come to Fort McMurray and spend some time with me. I thought he'd be safe if he got away for a while. He said he couldn't leave Heather and the kids."

"I'm sorry," Pete said. "Can you slow down? What did Nick need to get away from? Was he in some kind of trouble?"

"No, he wasn't in trouble. He was in danger. There's a world of difference between the two. Nicky knew someone was following him.

He didn't know who, and he didn't know why. He tried every way he could think of, that either of us could think of, to determine who and why." Cory's fists and jaw were clenched.

Pete and Martin exchanged glances.

Cory shook his head dejectedly. "I'm afraid I was no help at all. My only idea was that he come to Canada. I said they should all come—Nicky, Heather, and the kids. The unemployment rate is about four percent in and around Edmonton. That's why I'm there. There's such a need for qualified people. They're recruiting in the U.S. There's always a job for skilled and professional people, and the wages are outstanding. The tar sands, you know."

Cory exhaled deeply and continued. "Nicky insisted he couldn't relocate, because of Heather and the kids. What's going to happen to them now? If he makes it, God willing, I don't know if he'll be able to return to his job—or have a job to return to. Hank didn't go into it. For starters, if Nicky regains consciousness, after a brain injury like this, he'll have to learn to speak. The thoughts will be there, but he won't be able to express them."

Tears rolled down Cory's cheeks. He raised an arm, and wiped his face on his sleeve. He spent a minute composing himself before saying, "Even with insurance, the medical expenses will be astronomical. I'll do everything I can to help, but... I can't even think about it. Right now, the only important thing is Nicky."

The two investigators gave Cory time to talk about Nick and himself. When he'd talked himself out, Pete asked, "You live in both Fort McMurray and Edmonton?"

"I spend a couple of days each week in Fort McMurray. Otherwise I'm in Edmonton. Unfortunately, I was in Fort McMurray when Heather called. Otherwise I'd have been here yesterday."

"What do you do there?" Pete asked.

"I'm a safety engineer."

"Meaning?" Martin asked.

"I oversee the planning and review procedures and policies. My job is to ensure the infrastructure is in place to protect the workers. They're on the front line. They're making the money for the oil companies. They deserve to be protected."

"Protected from?" Martin asked.

"Against unsafe practices. Against any procedures that shortcut safety measures."

Pete switched gears, returning to their questions about Nick. "Did Nick tell Heather about his suspicions and fears?"

"He didn't. Said he couldn't. He wasn't willing to deal with her reaction—with the 'set of solutions she'd concoct.' Those are his exact words. Heather's a problem solver by vocation, and avocation. Nicky knew if she found a solution, even if he didn't like what it meant to his life, she wouldn't let go. He said she could be like a dog with a bone. He said he couldn't talk to her about it, until he had a plan. Don't get me wrong. He loves her dearly. He's demonstrated it in a hundred ways. I understand his viewpoint. Now I wish Nicky had told everyone about his suspicions, and damn the consequences! What if I'd ignored Nicky's wishes and told Heather? Maybe none of this would have happened. Maybe Heather could have done something." Cory broke down.

Once Cory composed himself, Pete said, "You can ask what ifs from here to eternity. That'll only make you crazy. It won't change anything."

Pete didn't mention his personal experience with that phenomenon. After pausing a moment, he reluctantly asked, "Nick was certain he was the only one in his family being stalked? That Heather and the kids weren't also in danger?"

"I can only surmise that Nicky was confident they weren't. I know he would have taken immediate action if he thought any of them were in danger."

Judging from their prior meetings, Cory was the only person Nick told about the stalker. Pete hoped that also made Cory a source for answers to many of the questions critical to solving the case. "When did your brother first tell you about his problem?" he asked.

"Nicky called me three weeks ago."

"Did he say when he started feeling like he was being followed?" Martin asked.

"Look, I don't want to be argumentative, but he didn't *feel* he was being followed. He *knew* it. It ought to be pretty obvious he was right. Unfortunately, I never asked when it started. I know it was quite some time before he told me. He'd been stewing for weeks." Cory sighed and shook his head.

"How did he know it?" Pete asked.

"I hate to say. If I do, you may decide he was imagining it. It should be obvious he wasn't. You don't think he was hit by accident, *do you?*"

"It doesn't look like an accident. It would help to know how he knew he was being followed," Pete said.

"He could feel it. Haven't you ever felt someone staring at you across a crowded room? I have, and I was right."

Pete was familiar with the feelings—and their accuracy. "You said he didn't know who was following him, or why," he said. "Determining that is our best route to finding this person. Can you think of any reason someone was after him?"

"No, Nicky and I talked about it. Hard as we tried, we couldn't answer that question."

"Did he have money problems?" Pete asked.

"Nicky was very careful with his money. Has always been. Became even more so after he was unemployed for more than a year. His and Heather's only debt is their mortgage."

"I am sorry to have to ask these questions," Pete said. "They're imperative. People who gamble often hide it from those they love…"

"Nicky isn't a gambler. I wanted him to bet fifty bucks on the World Series. He said he didn't need to have money on the games to enjoy them. He refused. I know that doesn't necessarily mean he isn't into other forms of gambling. He never buys pull tabs. He doesn't buy lottery tickets. He won't go to any of the casinos with me. All I can tell you is, I know him better than anyone. I'd never believe he has a gambling problem."

"This is an even touchier subject," Pete continued. "Did Nick have an affair—either current, or in the past?"

"No, absolutely not!" Cory shook his head decisively.

"Are you positive?" Pete asked.

"Yes!"

"And you can be positive because... ?" Martin asked.

"Because Nicky tells me everything, and I mean *everything*."

"But if Nick had an affair, regretted it, and didn't want it to affect his standing in your eyes, he..."

"He didn't want to bring himself down to my level?" Cory interrupted Martin. "Nicky saw what my affair did to my marriage and my kids. I can guarantee he didn't have an affair. I'd bet my last dollar!"

Changing the topic, but barely, Pete asked, "Is it possible that Heather had an affair or is having one?"

For the first time, Cory paused, carefully considering either the question or his answer.

TWENTY-FOUR

F inally, Cory opened his eyes, exhaled slowly and said, "If Heather's affair is the reason this happened, it will destroy her. It ended months ago. They had some tough times—some horrible fights. They got counseling, resolved their issues and got their marriage back on track. Heather's affair woke Nicky up. He realized she needed more from him. She needed more than a father for their kids. She needed to spend quality time with him. Nicky has lots of hobbies, and likes to go off by himself to enjoy them. He started including Heather and the kids. Before the stalking began, he was the happiest I've ever seen him. Perhaps I should say, the happiest I've ever heard him. We've talked every couple of weeks for as long as I can remember."

"Heather's affair ended last summer," Cory continued. "It couldn't explain what happened, could it? Seriously, who waits that long to get revenge? No one, right?"

Cory wanted reassurance.

The two investigators couldn't provide it. At this point, it was impossible to know the answer.

Pete mentioned the incidents at Locker's and on Nick's way to the Timberwolves game.

Cory knew about both.

Pete told him it meant the investigation was broader than Heather's affair.

Cory seemed to find comfort in that. It was short-lived.

"I should have caught the first plane out of Edmonton after Nicky told me someone was after him. I'm the only one who could have helped him. It's my fault he's fighting for his life." Cory's face dropped into his hands, and his back shook.

The two investigators waited silently. When Cory's back seemed to relax, Pete said, "Look, you gave him the option. It's probable, unless you knew who was after him, that the only way you could have prevented this was by coming here and dragging him back to Edmonton. Based on what you've told us, you'd have had to chain him down to keep him there. He'd have loved that, and it would have done wonders for your friendship. Also, as unlikely as it may seem right now, it's possible that the person who struck your brother had nothing to do with the stalker."

"Yeah." Cory took a deep breath and blew out his cheeks with the protracted exhalation. "I guess."

"Do you know the name of the person Heather was seeing?" Pete asked, careful not to make any assumptions about the person's gender.

"Nicky told me. I don't know the guy. His name is on the tip of my tongue." Cory stared into space, than looked back at Pete, shook his head and said, "Sorry, I can't think of it."

"Do you know anything else about the man? Where he works? Anything like that?" Martin asked.

"No, sorry. What else do you need from me?"

"How long will you be in town?" Pete asked.

"I'm not sure. At least a few weeks, I'd guess. It all depends on what happens, and how long I'm needed."

Both Pete and Martin handed Cory a business card. "We won't keep you, but call one of us when you think of that name," Pete said. "You can call me irrespective of the hour. If you fail to remember the name, is there someone you can ask?"

"Only Heather. I have no idea who else knows, and there's no way I'd ask her. Not now. I'll come up with it. I'll call as soon as I do. Plan on hearing from me no later than tomorrow. It's okay if it takes until tomorrow, isn't it?"

"Tomorrow's fine," Martin said. "The earlier the better. And call also if you think of anything else. Can we get you a ride somewhere?"

"No. Thanks. I'm sure Heather is still here. If not, I'll catch a cab. Besides, I want to spend some time with Nicky tonight. I want to give him a pep talk. He's unresponsive, but I believe he knows everything that's happening around him. Thanks for everything. I hope you set a land speed record when it comes to solving this one."

Pete smiled, and Martin nodded.

Walking to the unmarked, Pete said, "I suppose you want to get a drink or a burger and fries at Locker's before you head home."

Martin looked at him like he was crazy. "No, but I suppose you're hoping to be hit on by a young, infamous waiter."

"I'd thought about it, but decided I can control my passion. Maybe tomorrow? I'm exhausted."

"Me too, Pete. I've had about as much fun as I can stand for one day."

Driving home from headquarters, Pete thought about the latest twist in the investigation.

TWENTY-FIVE

By the time he walked through his back door, Pete felt better. It began with the decision to call Katie Benton. He wanted to give her a heads-up that it wasn't looking good for Saturday. Despite the reason for the call, the thought of talking to her lightened his mood. He went from there to thinking about some of their times together.

He thought about the first time he kissed her, on their first date. He was such a cad. That was so far-fetched that he broke into a smile. He thought about Katie's reaction to that kiss. Had he scripted it, he'd have written it exactly as it played out.

Pete thought about skiing with her at Spirit Mountain in Duluth. The view, skiing behind Katie and toward Lake Superior was awesome. The scenery wasn't bad, either. Hmm, maybe he was a cad.

They had a terrific time at the Great Minnesota Get Together, better known as the State Fair. Miraculously, he wasn't forced to give away the tickets to see Garrison Keillor's grandstand show. He and Katie loved it! He was sorry when Keillor decided to find a replacement host for *A Prairie Home Companion*. For him, the show, as much as "The News from Lake Wobegon," was Keillor. He couldn't imagine it with another host. He was delighted when Keillor shelved that plan.

He always had a good time with Katie. She endured his sense of humor and made him laugh. She was good for him.

Still, he was unconvinced the relationship could survive the demands of his career. Perhaps he needed to look at it from the other direction. Would his career survive marriage?

He loved the challenge, the adrenaline rush when he was in the heat of an investigation. Could he find that kind of satisfaction in another line of work? Did he want to?

Just as important, what did Katie think of their relationship? He knew she liked him—a lot. But did she like him enough to deal with his idiosyncrasies on a day-to-day basis? Would he ever get the nerve to broach the subject?

After going to his bedroom and changing into a worn pair of blue jeans and a T-shirt, Pete walked into the living room and sat in the recliner. He put up his feet and dialed Katie's number.

When Katie answered, Pete began by asking about her week.

"Is something wrong, Pete? You don't sound like yourself. Are you okay?"

"Yeah, I'm fine. Just tired. It's been a tough few days. So many questions. So few answers. That's part of the reason I called."

"Mind if I interrupt?"

"No. Go ahead."

"Do you want to get away for a while? Have you had dinner?"

"Not yet. I wanted to call you first."

"I could fix dinner for you. It will be ready by the time you arrive. You wouldn't have to stick around. We could talk while you eat, and you could leave right after you finish. Interested?"

"I'd love to, Katie. Seriously, I would. But I'm beat. I could fall asleep while eating. If you wanted to do me in, you could fix soup and let me drown."

"If I fix French onion, the bread and cheese might save your life. It's up to you, Pete. I'm happy to fix something, but I understand if you want to beg off."

"I think I should, but thanks. The reason I called was to say I've got a deal for you."

"I'm sitting, shoot. Sorry, that's my attempt at cop humor. What's up?"

Pete chuckled. "I thought I told you, never say 'shoot' to a cop. Anyway, you know our tickets for Saturday?"

"Yes?"

He explained the current investigation could prevent him from going to the History Theatre. He asked if she could find a friend to accompany her in the event he couldn't get away. Then he asked the latest he could let her know if he would make it.

Katie listened without a word. When he finished, she said, "The play starts at eight. How about calling my cell no later than seven thirty? I have a friend who lives within a few blocks of the theater. She's one of the few people I'd ask. I know she wouldn't mind playing second fiddle. We could sit tight at her place, and walk to the theater if you can't make it. How does that sound, Pete?"

"It works for me, but are you sure this friend will agree? I'd be less than thrilled with reserving the time and finding out at the last minute I was no longer invited."

"I agree. If you're able to make it on Saturday, I'll find a way to make it up to her."

"Okay. Thanks for being so understanding, Katie. And thanks again for the dinner offer.

"Don't give it a second thought. You're worth the wait."

Katie couldn't see Pete's blush.

"I'll call you Friday, or by noon on Saturday at the latest, to give you an update. It may not be any more informative than this conversation, but I'll do what I can, and you'll have a definite answer no later than seven thirty on Saturday. Take care. I'll be thinking about you."

"I'll be thinking about you, too, Pete, and looking forward to the next time I see you—whenever that happens."

Pete hung up. He was still smiling. Katie seemed too good to be true. Was she? He chastised himself. Thinking that way would get him nowhere fast. Worse yet, it could deep-six this relationship.

TWENTY-SIX

The next morning, Pete completed his run and prepared for work in record time. That placed him ahead of much of the rush hour traffic. It permitted him to avoid city streets and take I-35E to headquarters.

When Martin arrived, he was in his office, flipping through his notes and setting priorities for the day. "Let's go to Kevin Douglas's home," he said before Martin had a chance to remove his overcoat.

"Douglas should be at work by now," Martin puffed. He was already out of breath, trying to keep up with Pete, as he dashed to the parking lot.

"That's what I'm hoping. I want to question his mother, and I don't want him to interfere. If she worked last night, she got off at seven. She should be home by the time we get there. She said she keeps the same schedule when she does and doesn't work. This might be a good opportunity to test the veracity of that claim."

It wasn't. It took her a long time to answer the door. When she did, she wore a thick robe and warm slippers.

"We only need a minute," Pete explained. "Is Kevin here?"

"Come in, come in. I can't afford to heat all of St. Paul."

After he and Martin stepped inside, Pete closed the door and turned back to Murray.

"No, he's at work," she said. "I already told you he works Monday through Friday and starts at seven."

"Does he have a down jacket, parka, whatever?" Pete asked.

"Do you have a search warrant?"

Pete hated the way the overabundance of law enforcement programs on TV complicated his life. "No," he said, "but it's a simple yes-or-no question. I'm confused by your unwillingness to answer. It makes me think Kevin's been up to something. Guess we need to keep an eye on him. Thanks anyway."

He turned abruptly and reached for the doorknob.

"Okay, okay, *fine*. No, Kevin doesn't have a down jacket, and you don't need to make his life miserable. All this fuss is already making him irritable. *Please*, leave him alone."

"What fuss is that?" Pete asked.

"The fuss over his grandmother's stolen car."

"And?" Pete asked.

"That and having you go to Cambridge and harass him. That's all."

"Does he have a few more bucks these days?" Pete asked.

"No, why would he?"

"Just wondering if he found his dad, got a little money but an otherwise poor reception, and that's what's making him irritable," Pete said.

"Don't you think he'd have told me if he did?" she said, pouting and looking obstinate.

"You know him better than I. What do you think?" Pete asked.

Murray stared at him, not bothering to mask her revulsion.

This time Pete and Martin didn't feign their departure.

TWENTY-SEVEN

I understand asking about the jacket," Martin said. "Why did you ask if Douglas has more money? Are you thinking Nick Rice is his dad?"

"Just testing the waters, Martin. Per Cory, Nick hasn't had an affair, but this would have been before he married Heather. Rice would have been nineteen or twenty when Murray got pregnant. I thought maybe a poor reception from his dad or trying to kill him made Douglas irritable. Guess someone else will have to answer that question."

Walking to the car, Pete reached for and checked his cell phone. He had a text message from Cory Rice. It read, "Name u need: Paul V Norman. R E Agent. Vadnais Hts."

Foregoing an explanation, Pete thanked Martin for the *Yellow Pages* his partner carried in his unmarked. He hoped they would expedite the search for a phone number and address for Norman. He was amazed when he reached the desired section and saw pages and pages of real estate agencies in Vadnais Heights. He didn't think the suburb northeast of St. Paul was large enough to merit all those listings. Thank goodness Norman didn't work at a Minneapolis real estate office. He and Martin could have spent a month calling all those agencies.

Deciding there had to be a better way, he used his phone to look for a Paul V. Norman in Vadnais Heights. It stood to reason he'd have a listed number. Real estate agents wanted people to call, right?

In the process of entering the name, his curiosity was piqued. How did Cory know Norman's middle initial? It was one thing to remember the guy's name, but his middle initial? Did Cory get it from Heather? He made a mental note.

For whatever reason, the listings that came up covered the Twin Cities metropolitan area, not just Vadnais Heights. There was only one Paul V, but the results showed a long list of Paul Normans. Pete silently thanked Paul's parents for giving him an uncommon middle name, and Cory for including the initial in his text.

So much for printed directories. In no time flat, he had what he wanted.

He dialed the number.

A woman answered, "Paul V. Norman Realty."

Pete asked for Paul.

"I'm sorry, Paul isn't here. He'll be back late this morning or early this afternoon. Would you like to leave a message in his voicemail?"

"Oh, no! I misplaced his phone number." Pete glanced at his watch and continued, "It's almost nine o'clock. I was supposed to get back to him no later than nine. It's really important. Do you have another way I can reach him?"

The woman provided a cell phone number and claimed not to have a home number for Norman.

"Oh, for the good old, pre-cell phone days," Pete said as he disconnected.

"Seems like a strange comment, coming from a guy who just relied on his."

Pete called the number provided, and a pleasant voice answered on the second ring. He explained he was a St. Paul investigator and wanted to meet with Norman this morning.

When Norman said he had a full schedule for the next few days, Pete offered to camp out at his office until Norman could fit him in.

Norman harrumphed and recited his location. He warned they had until nine forty. He said he had to be out the door no later than that time.

The address was on St. Paul's East Side. His home was within a stone's throw of the parkway—so long as the person throwing the stone had Olympic potential. The house was ranch style with a two-story add-on.

Pete wondered if the add-on was built to accommodate Norman's livelihood. Did he have to get a variance? No doubt, but a real estate broker would know all the angles to accomplish that.

A quick calculation told Pete that Norman's home was less than a mile from the accident scene, within a half-mile of the Rice home, and no more than two miles from the Douglas/Murray residence.

Martin parked in the driveway, within inches of Norman's Mercedes. Turning to Pete, he smiled and said, "Leaving before we're finished with him will be a challenge for Paul V."

TWENTY-EIGHT

Norman nearly beat Pete and Martin to his front door. "What's this all about?" he demanded, glancing at their badges and IDs, then glaring at the two investigators.

Paul V. Norman had curly black hair in the early stages of the dreaded progression from forehead to crown. His ice-blue eyes were piercing.

Pete estimated his age as forty-five to fifty. He would verify that later.

"Where were you the day before yesterday, between five and eight in the morning?" Martin asked.

"I was here. I'm almost always here at that time."

Pete looked past Norman. The interior indicated more wealth than the home's exterior. *Unusual*, he thought, then remembered that the car Norman drove proclaimed his status.

Norman didn't offer a more comfortable location, so the questioning continued with all three men standing on the foyer tiles.

"Can anyone vouch for that?" Martin asked.

"My wife and my children can. I always try to have breakfast with them, since I often have evening appointments. That's when people usually want to look at homes, you know."

"We'd like to speak with your wife," Pete said.

"What's this all about?"

"No doubt you're aware of Nicholas Rice's accident," Pete said.

"Of course. Only a hermit could live this close to the accident and not know about it. What does that have to do with me? Surely you don't think I'm responsible."

"I didn't hear anyone say we think he's responsible. Did you, Martin?"

"Nope. What do you think, Commander? Does it sound like his conscience is playing tricks on him?"

"Look, things are already uncomfortable around here. I don't need any more problems. Is this really necessary?"

"How about if we save you some time? Tell us where your wife works and her phone number. We'll handle it," Pete said.

Without a word, Paul Norman got a phone and began dialing. As he did, Pete said, "I'm confident you're not foolish enough to say anything to influence her answers."

When Norman's wife answered, he said, "Jill, I have someone here who wants to talk to you." He placed the phone in Pete's outstretched hand.

Pete explained who he was, and that he was investigating the hit-and-run involving Nicholas Rice.

If Jill Norman recognized the name or wondered why Pete was at her home, she didn't say. She outlined their schedule yesterday morning. "We got up at six thirty. Paul fixed breakfast while I showered. He always fixes breakfast, since I have to leave before he does."

Pete was confident Norman could have gotten home from the accident scene before six thirty, even if he wasn't a runner. If intentional, would Norman select a place so close to home—a place where he might be recognized? Sure, by all appearances the number of people who'd heard the accident and checked it out was three: two residents and him. But wouldn't a guy planning a hit be overly cautious?

Well, not always. There were plenty of examples of people being reckless—or stupid.

Pete asked if Jill was certain Paul was home between five and six thirty. She admitted waking up at four, but going back to sleep and not waking up until the alarm started buzzing at six thirty.

In response to the next question, yes, she was a sound sleeper.

"What kind of car do you drive, Ms. Norman?"

"A Chrysler 300."

"What year?"

"2011."

"And the color?"

"White. Chrysler calls it ivory tri-coat pearl."

"Any cars in the family besides yours and your husband's?"

"Yes, my son's. Actually, it's ours, but we let him use it."

"What kind of car?" Pete asked.

"A Toyota Camry."

"What color is the Camry?" Pete asked.

"It's midnight blue."

Pete didn't bother to get any other details on the Toyota. He could readily get them later. He thanked Jill and handed the phone back to Paul.

Paul hung up without checking to see if Jill was still on the line.

"How old are your kids?" Pete asked.

"Sixteen and eighteen."

"Which is your son?" Martin asked.

"Dylan's eighteen."

"Describe your son," Martin said.

"He's my height, five-ten or thereabouts, he's about 170 pounds, black curly hair, blue eyes. I often hear that he looks just like me. He's on the varsity football and baseball teams. He's a star running back. I think he'll get a full ride at a Big Ten school. Maybe even Nebraska or Penn State."

"So he's fast," Pete said.

"You'd better believe it. Ran the forty-yard dash in 4.32 seconds," Norman bragged.

"Impressive." Pete nodded.

"What's your daughter's name?" Martin asked.

"Caitlin."

"Where do Dylan and Caitlin go to school?" Pete asked.

"Anderson Senior High."

"I understand you and Heather Rice are close," Pete said.

"I haven't seen or spoken with her in more than six months." Norman clenched his jaw and glowered.

"She got tired of you?" Pete asked.

"No."

"Are you sure?" Pete asked.

"I'm positive." Norman looked like he wanted to strangle Pete.

"And you're positive because... ?" Pete asked.

"Because my wife's the one who ended it."

"And how did she do that?" Pete asked.

"With an ultimatum."

"Did your kids find out? I know something like that can really hurt a guy's relationship with his kids," Pete said.

"Yes, they know," Norman muttered.

"How did they react?" Pete asked.

"Both sided with my wife and were angry with me."

"How angry?" Pete asked.

"Not angry enough to attack Heather Rice, much less her husband. My take on it is that Jill convinced the kids it was all my fault."

"Are things back to normal? That is, do you think your son and daughter have gotten over it or are coping better?"

"Yes, things are definitely back to normal for the kids. Jill and I are coping. It was mighty uncomfortable around here for a while, but it's okay now."

"When did you, Jill, and your kids first reach the current state of normalcy and coping?" Pete asked.

"Around Christmas, I'd say. I think the holiday spirit helped."

"Do you, Jill, or your kids have down parkas?" Pete asked.

"Yes, we all have them. We have a couple of snowmobiles. What does that have to do with anything?"

"You tell me," Pete said.

"I have no idea. In fact, I think this is a fishing expedition. I just don't get what you're fishing for."

"What colors are those jackets?" Martin asked.

"You're kidding me, right?"

"Couldn't be more serious," Martin said.

"They're black, navy, powder blue, and yellow."

"Okay, tell me who has which color," Martin said.

"Mine's black. My son's is navy. My wife's is yellow, and my daughter's is blue. Are you looking for ways to waste my time, or is it coincidental?"

"You and your son are the same size?" Martin asked.

"Pretty much."

"So his jacket fits you and vice versa?" Martin asked.

"Yes, and my wife and daughter are about the same size. So what?"

"What time does your son get up for school?" Martin asked.

"About the same time or a little earlier than my wife and me."

"And your daughter?" Martin asked.

"Six thirty or a little earlier, like the rest of us. Dylan drives to school. They're both on a fast track to shower and get out the door."

"Where are the bedrooms?" Martin asked.

"All three are down that hallway," Norman said, pointing toward the east side of his home.

"Where are you sleeping these days?" Pete asked.

Norman's face turned scarlet. "With my wife. Thanks for your concern." Norman sneered.

"I see you built an addition. How do you use the extra space?" Pete asked.

"It's my office. Why?"

"With your hours, I'll bet you sometimes doze off in your office," Pete said.

"No, never. It isn't that far from my office to the bedroom. Why would I want to wake up with a stiff neck?"

TWENTY-NINE

Approaching Wheelock Parkway, Pete asked Martin to pull over while he called Locker's Bar and Grill. "If Locker's opens for lunch, I think staff will be there by now," he explained.

Pete called the number he'd written in his notebook and got a recorded message. "Open for lunch," he said. "Let's go."

"By the way," Martin said, "Been meaning to tell you, Marty told me Wheelock Parkway was named for Joseph Albert Wheelock. He founded the *St. Paul Pioneer Press*. I'd joked that I thought it was named after Wheelock Whitney. Marty went online and set me straight. I'm amazed at what that kid can do with a computer. I could raise his allowance in exchange for him researching the history of all of our crime scenes. That information would make me a valuable asset to the department, don't you think?" Martin smiled.

"Definitely, if you're spelling that ass-E-T-T-E." Pete laughed.

Martin couldn't help himself. He laughed, too.

The two investigators didn't find the owner or a manager at Locker's. They did find someone who remembered the incident the night of the Regisson party.

"The guy who blew up was a jerk!" the waitress said. "Ron treats all the women that way. I do it with the guys. We have to be friendly, no matter how disgusting the patron is. We depend on tips, you know. I'll bet the guy wouldn't have had a problem if I was flirting with him."

"Did Ron lose his job?" Pete asked.

"No. He probably would have if the old manager, I mean the previous manager, was still here. However, he was told if anything like that ever happens again, he's out the door. Unbelievable!"

"Is Ron here today?" Pete asked.

"Not yet. He starts at six."

"Is that his usual shift?" Pete asked.

"Yes."

"Did he work the last three nights?" Martin asked.

"I think so. Let me check." She returned a minute later with the laminated schedule. "See his name is here, here, and here." Her index finger jabbed at the cited locations. "Same shift all three days," she added, smiling at Pete, then Jack.

Pete noted that the schedule also showed Ron working until two in the morning, apparently allowing him time to help clean up after they closed.

"What's his last name?" Pete asked.

"Marshall."

"Describe Ron," Pete said.

"Best guess, he's an inch or two taller than you," she said, assessing Pete. "He's muscular and has a gorgeous head of jet-black hair. He's very sweet, and women love it when he hits on them."

"What kind of car does he drive?" Pete asked.

"A Jeep"

"Which model?" Pete asked.

"I don't know. I thought I was doing well to know it's a Jeep." She giggled.

"What color?" Pete asked.

"Canary yellow with black trim."

"What year?" Pete asked.

"I have no idea." She raised her shoulders and palms.

"A guy Ron's size could do a lot of damage to a guy the size of the man who got upset with him the night of the Regisson party," Pete said.

"Ron would never hurt anyone. He's a pussycat. He's the gentlest man I know."

THIRTY

Pete called the Crime Lab regarding their investigation of the 1991 Buick LeSabre. The car was at the impound lot and could sit there until the case was closed. By then, the costs to the owner, between towing and storage, could approach the national debt. At least it would feel that way to Vera Lyon. It was a given those costs would exceed the pre-accident value of the LeSabre—many times over. Pete felt sorry for people like Vera who, through no fault of their own, found themselves in this predicament.

Two different types of hair were found in the LeSabre. The DNA had not yet been analyzed. That information wouldn't be available for minimally a week and more likely a few weeks. Pete wasn't put off by the delay. The hairs likely belonged to Kevin and his grandmother. If so, their identification contributed nothing to the investigation.

Fibers of a material used for the outer shell of ski jackets and ski pants were found. Unfortunately, the use of this material was widespread, so the fibers would be useful only when a jacket or ski pants were provided to analyze for a match.

If alcohol was a contributing factor, there were no signs of that in the LeSabre.

"Let's talk to Kevin's grandmother and her neighbors," Pete said. "Kevin's mother says he doesn't have a down parka. I want to know if anyone has seen him wearing one."

The two investigators had a good look at Vera Lyon's home as they walked up the steps to her front door.

Pete and Martin showed her their IDs and she looked carefully at them.

"Sorry. I'm such a 'fraidy cat, ever since my car was stolen. I used to be trusting, not anymore." She smiled sheepishly.

She was short, only a shade over five feet, slender, and ramrod straight. She wore a sweatsuit, possibly fending off the cold.

When she invited the investigators into her home, the reason for the sweatsuit was clear. She must have the heat turned down to conserve money, Pete thought. Or perhaps she's going green.

Vera's home was modestly but tastefully decorated and immaculate. It appeared that she lived by a saying often recited by his grandmother: "A place for everything, and everything in its place." The walls were papered with delicate prints, and she had crocheted doilies on the arms of the chairs and sofa. A variety of fragile knick-knacks decorated every flat surface.

Pete smiled. She looked like the stereotypical grandmother, and her home supported that appraisal. She reminded him so much of his maternal grandmother that he almost, reflexively, bent down and hugged her. He practiced restraint.

"We're sorry about your LeSabre, ma'am," Pete said.

"Vera, my name is Vera. Did you come about my LeSabre?"

"Actually, we're wondering about Kevin Douglas," Pete said. "From what we've heard, he's a wonderful grandson."

"I don't know what I'd do without Kevin. He does so much for me."

"I think I saw him going around the corner when we drove up," Pete said. "This guy was the right size and his hair looked like Kevin's. He was wearing a down parka. The parka was black or navy. On an overcast day like today, I can't always distinguish between the two. Was that Kevin?"

"I know what you mean about black and navy, but you seem awfully young to be having that problem. I've never seen him in a down jacket. He doesn't have one—unless it's brand new. The person you saw couldn't have been Kevin. If he was in the neighborhood, he'd have stopped to say 'hi,' even if he only had a minute."

"Has Kevin changed his schedule in the last several weeks?" Pete asked. "What I mean is, has he been available less often or not at the usual times?"

"No, he's always available when I need him. A couple of times he even used his vacation hours to take me to appointments."

"I understand Kevin has been upset or irritable for a while. Have you noticed that, too?" Pete asked.

"Poor Kevin. He's been upset ever since my car was stolen. I told him to forget it, that it isn't his fault. That doesn't seem to help. I'm afraid he feels responsible."

"Why would he feel responsible?" Martin asked.

"I don't really know. He hasn't said. I wonder if he thinks he might not have locked the doors. I've always wished I had a garage."

"The thing is, whether or not the doors are locked usually only makes a difference of a few seconds. It often doesn't keep the car from being stolen," Pete said.

"Has Kevin been especially tired lately?" Martin asked.

"Yes, and again, I think it's because my car was stolen. I don't think he's sleeping these days."

"How about the week or two before your car was stolen? Was he unusually tired then as well?" Martin asked.

"I don't think so. Why would he be?"

"Your daughter said he's been looking for his father, Vera. Has Kevin asked you about him?" Martin asked.

"Kevin asks everyone about his father. It's become an obsession. Do you blame him?"

"Do you think he has any idea who it might be?" Pete asked.

"My daughter and I don't discuss those things."

"How about Kevin? Has he said anything to make you think he's making progress with his search?" Pete asked.

"No, he hasn't." Vera sounded less accommodating.

"Did you ever think anyone was hanging around your car, Vera?" Pete asked. "You know what I mean—looking in the windows or walking around it, checking it out?"

"Not that I noticed, but that doesn't mean much. I didn't spend time looking out at it. I only do that now that it's gone. You know, I keep hoping one of these times I'll look out the window, and there it will be, good as new." She smiled longingly.

"You didn't pay much attention to your car," Pete said. "That's understandable. How about people? Do you pay attention to the people around here?"

"It all depends. I do in the summer, when I'm gardening. Not so much this time of year. I assume you're referring to this winter."

"In the last few weeks, when you noticed the people outside, did you see any unfamiliar people hanging around?" Pete asked.

"No, I didn't notice anyone like that."

Pete pulled up stock photos of the three cars owned by the Norman family and showed them one by one to Vera. She inspected them carefully, but didn't recognize any of them.

"We're wondering if any of your neighbors might have seen something," Pete said. "Are any of them home this time of day?"

"Most of my neighbors are my juniors by a decade or more, but many are retired. Can't say if they'll be home, though."

Pete and Martin thanked Vera and sought out her neighbors.

Pete took the west side of Vera's street, and Martin took the east side. Several neighbors knew who Kevin was and some saw him on a regular basis on his way into and out of his grandmother's home, and when he took her on errands.

None of them had seen Kevin in a black or dark-colored down jacket or hooded jacket of any kind. The few who had spoken with him since Christmas didn't think he was more nervous or agitated, nor had they observed any other changes in his personality. None of them remembered seeing any of the Norman family vehicles parked in the neighborhood.

Pete asked about the Honda Accord parked across the street from Vera's home. It faced Wheelock Parkway and would have provided the fastest trip to the crash scene. Several neighbors confirmed that the Accord belonged to the person who owned the house where it was parked. That woman was said to have owned it forever. Like Vera's vehicle, it was rarely driven, and always parked on the street in front of the owner's home.

"Aha, no wonder you're so interested in the Accord," Martin said when he and Pete shared their findings. "Why would somebody steal a boat like a 1991 LeSabre when a Honda Accord is right across the street? Why would the thief want a LeSabre?"

"I've been mulling that over. It suddenly occurred to me that a 1991 LeSabre is ideal, if the driver doesn't want to have the escape hindered by airbags. Only thing is, the Accord belonging to her neighbor is also pre-airbags. There's a reason the LeSabre was the vehicle of choice, but right now I'm stumped. Can you ask your matrix about it?"

"If I do, I can't share the answer with you. My matrix is adverse to helping nonbelievers." Martin smiled.

THIRTY-ONE

P ete's cell vibrated. The name on the caller ID was Cory Rice.
"Commander, I want to help find the person who did this to Nicky. How about if I put up a 10,000 dollar reward with Crime Stoppers?"

"Crime Stoppers might be an option down the road, Cory, but not yet. It's too soon. It's more useful when an investigation is going nowhere. If and when the time is right, I'll let you know and link you up with them. While I've got you, my partner and I want to meet with Heather and her children. We prefer to speak with them as a group, at least initially. I realize this will be difficult for them, but it's critical to the investigation."

"Can it wait a few days?"

"We've already postponed it a few days."

"I understand. Heather's been camping out at the hospital. She's here now. She's getting cleaned up and packing some fresh clothes before she heads back. Hang on."

Heather got on the phone, and Pete arranged to meet with her as soon as he and Martin could reach her home.

When they arrived, they met with Heather and her children in the living room. The expressions on their faces suggested each one expected this meeting to be the next worst thing to Nick's accident.

Body language painted a similar picture. The children sat stiffly in a row on the couch. Their proximity to one another seemed peculiar for siblings their age. Pete wondered if they felt vulnerable, thanks to the events of the week.

Alexis was petite. She was a blonde Shirley Temple, and looked more like ten than twelve. Pete wondered if she paid a price for that. Kids her age could be brutal.

Both boys looked rough and tumble—like their favorite state was dirty.

Heather repeatedly rearranged her position on the overstuffed chair where she settled. Those movements seemed to indicate that she couldn't get comfortable. Pete wondered if she was waiting for the other shoe to drop. Did she know or suspect that Cory told them about her affair?

Their conversation with Sybil Wright gave Pete and Martin a general idea of the layout of the Rice home and yard. Sitting in the living room, Pete looked out the picture window in the formal dining room. With the bare tree branches, he had an unobstructed view of downtown St. Paul, courtesy of the drop-off behind the Rice home.

Sybil said she saw someone go through the yards and head down that hill. Pete wondered if that person could see in as well as he now saw out.

The condition of the living room and its furnishings suggested the room was entered only when an abundance of flourishing plants were watered.

Heather began, "I want to tell you how much we appreciate everything you did for Nick, Commander Culnane. I was told you're the person who found him and called 911. I understand you did everything possible to help him. Words can't begin to express our gratitude."

Three young heads with three forlorn faces nodded. Tears dropped silently to three small laps.

"I'm glad I was nearby and could get to your dad right away," Pete said, looking from one child to the next. "Now my partner, Sergeant Tierney, and I are doing everything we can to find the person who did this. That's why we're here. First, I want to make sure you understand one thing: For all we know, the car hit your dad accidentally. Those things happen a lot. Know what I mean?"

All three kids stared solemnly at Pete and nodded.

Pete hated when his job demanded this sort of thing. Trying to minimize the pain for these young victims of a senseless act, he continued, "Despite that, we have to look at other possibilities. Does that make sense?"

Three more nods.

"All we need is your answers to a few questions. Will you answer my questions?"

Three small faces glanced at their mother, then nodded, hesitantly.

"Great. Did you ever see someone you don't know hanging around your house or the neighborhood?"

Two small wide-eyed heads shook back and forth. One head nodded slowly.

"Sometimes I wake up really early. When I do, I may look outside to see how dark it is and check what I can see. Do you ever do that?"

One head nodded.

"I've found that things look very different early in the morning, when it's still dark outside. Have you ever noticed that?"

The same head nodded.

"Thanks for your help. I hope I haven't scared you. We believe you're safe. Our job is to keep you safe. We depend on you to help us with that. You can do that by telling your mom if you see something that scares you. Will you do that?"

Three grim-faced heads nodded.

"Okay, that's all we have for now. Do you have any questions?"

Three heads shook back and forth.

"How about something that might help us? Can you think of anything that might help us?"

Two heads shook. One nodded.

THIRTY-TWO

Thanks Alexis, Tyler, Danny." Heather gave a group hug to her three children. "I want to talk to these men a bit longer," she continued. "Alexis, would you please ask Aunt Sarah to put some cookies on a plate and bring them to me?"

"But, Mom, you never let anyone eat in the living room," eight-year-old Danny protested.

"I think it's okay to make this one exception. Go ahead, Alexis. Danny and Tyler, you can have cookies, too, but only two each, and you have to eat them in the kitchen. Sarah will get them for you."

After her children left, Heather moved across the room and sat on a loveseat. It was perpendicular to, and within whispering distance of, the two investigators. That location gave her a clear view of both passages into the living room. Once there, she thanked Pete for not asking Alexis for details while the boys were still in the room.

She spoke softly, while monitoring both doorways. "I'm worried about Alexis. She isn't herself. None of us are, but she's doing much worse than the rest of us. She and Nick are close. I'm sure that's part of it, but I think it's more than that. When she returns, I'll try to get her to talk. I've asked her repeatedly if there is something I can do to help. She only shakes her head and cries. I saw her nod in answer to some of your questions, Commander Culnane. That's a lot further than I've gotten with her. I think she may have nodded and said nothing to protect her brothers—to avoid scaring them. That would be very much like..."

Heather stopped speaking when Alexis appeared in the doorway. "Alexis," she said, "bring the cookies here. Then sit here next to me."

Alexis did as requested. After sitting as close as she could get to her mother, she concentrated on her clenched fists.

"Alexis," Heather said, "these gentlemen wonder if you thought of something that might help."

"I saw a man in the backyard," Alexis whispered, crouching forward and talking fast. Her eyes were fixed on Pete, as though this was their secret.

"When did you see this man, Alexis?" Pete asked.

"Last Wednesday, a week ago yesterday. He stood in the backyard, staring at our house. If I'd told Dad, maybe he wouldn't have been hurt. What if Dad dies?" Alexis's hands came to and covered her mouth. Her body was racked with muffled sobs.

Heather put an arm around her and held her close.

"Alexis," Pete said, "I've been a police officer for a very long time. If there's one thing I know, it's that you aren't responsible for what happened. The person who did it is responsible. No one else. Even if the person you saw was the person who drove the car, it isn't your fault. To say it's your fault is no more true than saying it was your dad's fault for not getting out of the way. Do you blame your dad for what happened?"

Alexis shook her head frantically.

"Me neither. Can you tell us why you think this person was a man? Did you see his face?" Pete asked.

Alexis shook her head apologetically.

"But you believe this was a man because… ?" Pete asked.

"He was big, like a man, and he wore a man's jacket."

"Can you describe the jacket?" Pete asked.

"It was a dark-colored down jacket—the kind that has fur around the edge of the hood. It went almost to his knees. I'm not positive about the color. It's dark in the backyard at night."

"Was the person wearing the hood?" Pete asked.

Alexis nodded.

"Suppose your mom put on a jacket like the one you saw. Would she look like that person?" Pete asked.

"I guess, but it wasn't you, Mom. Was it?"

Heather shook her head.

"What time did you see this person, Alexis?" Pete asked.

"It was a little after five thirty. I was still tired, and wanted to know if I had more time to sleep. After I looked at the clock, I thought I heard a noise in the backyard. So, I looked out the window."

"You're doing terrific, Alexis. Just a few more questions," Pete said. "Did you see this person leave?"

Alexis shook her head. "He scared me. As soon as I saw him, I ran back to bed, and pulled the covers over my head."

"I know you didn't get a clear view, due to the darkness, but do you think you might've seen this person before that night or since then?" Pete asked.

"I don't think so."

"Some people can tell the make and model of any car, but many people, including me, can't." Pete smiled. "Can you distinguish a Ford from a Chevrolet, a Honda from a Toyota?"

"Usually. Dad taught me." She looked forlorn.

"Wow, I'm impressed! Do you notice the cars around here?"

"Sometimes. Not always. Depends on the car."

Pete pulled up his photo of Kevin Douglas's car. Leaning to his left, he handed her his phone and said, "How about this one? Have you seen it around here?"

"I used to see a lot of cars just like this one. Not so many anymore. I don't know the last time I saw one or where I saw it. Sorry." She frowned.

Pete showed her a stock photo of Dylan Norman's car.

"I've seen a lot of cars like that one, too. So many that I can't tell you where. If it was pink, I'd know."

Pete nodded. "Okay, if you saw a pink car parked in front of your house, would you know if it was a Honda or a Toyota?"

Alexis smiled. "Yes! I'd wonder who made a pink car. I'd definitely look at the emblem."

Pete was pleased to see her smile. Hoping he was on a roll, he pulled up a photo of Paul Norman's car, then a stock photo of Jill Norman's car.

The only one she reacted to was the Chrysler 300. She saw it, or one like it, but she didn't know if she saw it parked on their street.

"I love that color," she said.

"Do you pay attention if an unusual car that isn't pink is parked in front of your house or on your street?" he asked.

"Like the Chrysler you just showed me?"

"Yes, but also cars like the first two I showed you."

"Sometimes."

"And that depends upon... ?" Pete asked.

"It depends on what I'm doing."

"Glad to hear you're normal." Pete laughed. "Alexis, I can't think of any other questions. If I think of some later, is it okay if I come back?"

Alexis smiled and nodded.

"Now we have a few questions for your mom," Pete said.

Alexis settled back on the loveseat. She seemed anxious to hear what they asked her mom.

Heather had other ideas. "Alexis, why don't you check on your brothers? I'm sure they're wondering what happened to you. You can tell them we were talking. Please don't tell them what you saw."

"Don't worry, Mom, I'd *never* do that."

"That's what I thought. Thanks, Alexis." She hugged her daughter, then kissed her forehead.

Heather hadn't seen anyone unusual or unfamiliar around the house or the neighborhood. She hadn't noticed any unfamiliar cars. She did want to tell the two investigators about her affair with Paul Norman.

Looking everywhere but at Pete and Martin, she said, "In *Fatal Attraction*, the girlfriend went after the wife. Do you think this could be some weird twist on that theme, Commander Culnane, Sergeant Tierney?"

"We're looking at everything, including your relationship with Norman," Martin said. "In your opinion, was he angry or upset enough about the end of your relationship to do something like this?"

"No, I'd be shocked." Heather looked uncomfortable.

"How about his wife?" Martin asked.

"She was furious when she found out. If she did something drastic, I think she'd do it to Paul, not me. Why would she go after Nick? That doesn't make any sense."

"Lots of times these things don't make sense. Is there anything else you can think of?" Martin asked. "Anything Nick did or said that surprised you? Any telephone hang-ups, or more hang-ups than usual? Any threatening calls? Anything at all?"

"We have caller ID. If I don't recognize the name or number, I ignore the call. With that qualification, the answer is no. I really can't think of anything. Do you think Nick thought he was in danger and didn't tell me?"

"Would he do that?" Pete asked.

"I don't think so."

"He may have suspected something, but not been sure, and maybe he was working on a solution," Pete said. "If either is true, it's possible he didn't want to alarm you. Do you have any other questions?"

"Are the children and I in danger?"

"We have no reason to believe so. If we did, or if that situation changes, we'll see that you have protection," Pete said. "Anything else?"

"Nothing I can think of. Not for now, anyway."

"I want to leave you with the same assurance we gave Alexis," Pete said. "You can't accept responsibility for what happened, regardless of who did it or why. Don't dig yourself into that hole."

Staring at the floor, Heather nodded.

Pete checked the time as he and Martin walked toward the unmarked.

"School's out," he said. "As long as we're here, let's see if we can find some kids who are into cars—kids who are longing for a car and trying to find one they can afford or get their parents to buy for them."

"The Wright woman mentioned the Polk kids," Martin said. "There's a small black car in their driveway. Since they drive a small black car, they might pay more attention to other small dark-colored cars."

It was a good idea, but it fell flat. The most the Polk kids had to offer was the houses where other neighborhood kids lived. The only vehicle recognized by any of those kids was Paul Norman's. None of them remembered seeing it after school started last fall. One kid suggested they talk to Sybil Wright.

Not a single kid saw a stranger lurking. Not one saw activity around the Rice home last week Wednesday, last Monday, or the day Nicholas Rice was struck.

Again, Pete and Martin headed for the unmarked. This time, they had the names and addresses of the neighborhood kids who weren't yet home from school.

THIRTY-THREE

Feels like our day to speak with neighbors. What do you think about talking to the Norman family's neighbors next, Martin?"

"Guess it's as good a time as any."

Again, they split up. Each canvassed one side of the street for several blocks. They spoke with everyone they found home. By the time they finished, they'd talked to a majority of the residents, and they had a list of the addresses where no one answered.

During this process, the two investigators got a detailed and perhaps skewed picture of the Norman family. Sitting in the unmarked car, they compared notes.

Neighbors pegged Jill as hardworking, based in part on the hours she left for and returned from work. That also meant some neighbors, especially the older ones, wondered who cooked dinner. They said she was polite but distant, and a no-nonsense woman. She participated in a variety of groups, including a book club and her church choir. She was physically active, especially in the summer when she rode her bike and golfed.

Paul was deemed more social and relaxed than Jill. The fact he rarely left for work before nine thirty might drive those opinions. Since the kids and Jill did all the yard work and shoveling, some assumed he lacked ambition. His hours led to some speculation he had a girlfriend. By all indications, the story hadn't hit the neighborhood grapevine.

Paul and Jill's daughter, Caitlin, rode to school with her brother, Dylan. They left a little after seven. Caitlin, a sophomore, was a straight-A student. A neighbor said she was on her school's cross-country team. He sometimes saw her running when he went out to get his morning paper. Caitlin was described as energetic, motivated, and determined. The neighborhood kids loved it when she babysat.

Dylan was a senior. He was a star on the varsity football and baseball teams. His grades were average. Neighbors speculated that was because studying took a backseat to sports. He was shy and unassuming, but a friendly kid who was always ready to lend a helping hand.

None of the neighbors noticed activity around the Norman house before six thirty in the morning on Tuesday, the day Rice was struck. That was also true of last week Wednesday, when Alexis Rice saw someone in her backyard, and Sybil Wright saw someone headed in that direction.

No one observed personality changes in any member of the Norman family. When the two investigators finished their assessment, it was almost seven.

"We should talk to the Normans," Martin said. "If we do it right, one of the kids might be helpful."

"Out of the mouths of babes?"

"Yeah. Let's do it now. We're here, and with the possible exception of Paul, they should all be home. Tomorrow morning, by the time we get here, the kids will be in school."

"I agree with you on all counts. But maybe before we go visit with the Normans, we should pick up a couple of collapsible chairs. What do you think, Martin?"

"If Paul's home, we'll probably regret not doing that." Martin smiled. "Do you think his wife will keep us standing in the foyer?"

"Can you imagine the look on Paul Norman's face if we showed up with our own chairs? It would be priceless. But it might not compete with the look on the faces in accounting when we include collapsible chairs on our expense reports."

THIRTY-FOUR

Neighbors described Paul as more affable than his wife. Pete wondered what to expect from Jill. Before long, he knew. She answered the doorbell.

Jill Norman had blonde hair pulled back and fastened with a butterfly clip. Her makeup was impeccably applied, but failed to conceal the lines around her mouth and eyes. She wore a bulky beige sweater that, if necessary, was capable of hiding a few pounds.

Jill said that neither Dylan nor Paul were home.

Pete explained that he and Martin had some questions for all four of them, and asked when she expected them.

"Dylan is studying with friends, and won't be home until about ten. I don't know about Paul."

She invited Pete and Martin in and led them toward the living room. As they passed the formal dining room, Pete requested they go there instead. The lighting and arrangement of the furniture in that room would make it possible to closely observe both Jill and Caitlin, when they spoke with the girl.

Jill and the two investigators took seats at a large, modern table. The matching buffet overflowed with cut glass and a sterling silver tea set. A crystal chandelier hung low over the table.

No telltale smells lingered to indicate if Jill and her family ate dinner here.

Jill sat, pulled her chair close to the table, and placed her hands on her lap. She smiled and waited for a hint about the reason for their return.

"No doubt you're aware of the hit-and-run that involved Nicholas Rice," Pete began.

"Yes, of course." Jill nodded. "It happened right in our neighborhood. That poor family."

"Yes, I agree," Pete said. "At the same time, if I were you, I'd find some satisfaction in knowing Heather Rice is paying for her transgressions. Don't you agree?"

"No!" Jill was up and out of her chair. Her previously placid expression was now a scowl. "I don't have to listen to this."

"You do have to answer our questions, either here or at headquarters," Pete said. "Would you prefer that we move the questioning to headquarters?"

"No," Jill said softly and sat down. "I don't blame Heather Rice for what happened. I know Paul. I blame him. And what kind of twisted mind would attack the spouse? That would mean I'm in danger, due to Paul's transgressions. Give me a break! That would be nonsense!"

"I understand Nicholas Rice found out about the affair and brought it to a screeching halt," Pete said.

"You're right about a spouse causing it to end. You have the wrong spouse."

"Is that your husband's opinion, also?" Pete asked.

"I assume so. I was very clear about my position."

"It sounds like this wasn't your husband's first affair. Was it?" Pete asked.

"I suspect not, but this is the first time I could prove it."

"Where were you between five and seven on Tuesday morning?" Pete asked.

"I told you that the last time we spoke. I was here until seven thirty."

"Tell us about your kids," Martin said.

Jill looked relieved to be moving to a more pleasant line of questioning. "Dylan is eighteen. He plays football and baseball. He's an average student and a good kid. He's honest, loving, sensitive, and respectful—most of the time. He is a teenager."

"How about your daughter?" Martin asked.

"Caitlin is always on the honor roll. She's hoping to get into Stanford. She's smart and works hard. She's already decided she'll be a medical doctor. She wants to concentrate on research. She's intent on finding a cure for Alzheimer's. I'm confident she'll succeed. When she sets a goal, there's no stopping her." Jill's smile exuded pride.

"Does she play any sports?" Martin asked.

"Lacrosse and basketball."

"How about cross country?" Martin asked. "Is she a cross-country runner or skier?"

"Not anymore."

"Which did she do, and when did she quit?" Martin asked.

"She was a cross-country runner. She didn't quit. She took up lacrosse instead."

"Is she running these days?" Martin asked.

"Yes."

"When does she run?" Martin asked.

"I think it depends on her schedule. Caitlin's independent, has been forever."

"Would you know if your daughter was getting up before dawn, going outside, and running?" Martin asked.

"I might hear her, and I might not. It would all depend on the time."

"Do you and your daughter talk?" Martin asked.

"Yes, of course. We're a close family."

"Would your daughter tell you if she was upset or angry?" Martin asked.

"It depends on how upset or angry, and the reason she felt that way. Did you tell your parents everything when you were sixteen?" Jill looked like she thought Martin was stupid.

Martin was unaffected. "How about your son? How's his emotional state these days?" he asked.

"Good. He's a teenage boy. He wants more freedom. He rebels."

"Has he been more rebellious in the last few weeks or days?" Martin asked.

"No."

"Has he been more tired?" Martin asked.

"He's always tired. I can't get him to go to bed at night or get up in the morning."

"Have you noticed any changes in your husband or your kids?" Martin asked.

"I don't understand what you're asking."

"Is anyone more depressed, angry, upset? Anything like that?" Martin asked.

"No, nothing has changed. Everything and everyone is the same."

"Who had the strongest reaction to your husband's affair with Heather Rice?" Pete asked.

"I did, of course. Paul and I both did our best to hide it from our children."

"Did you succeed?" Pete asked.

"Not completely."

"Meaning?" Pete asked.

"Meaning I had a meltdown one night, and the kids heard us."

"How long ago was that?" Martin asked.

"I'm not sure."

"What's your best guess?" Martin asked.

"Early November, I guess."

"That had to have an impact on your kids," Martin said.

"Of course it did."

"And they were angrier or more sullen or moodier after that?" Martin asked.

"For a day or two, I guess."

"That's all?" Martin asked.

"*Yes!*"

"They must be unusually resilient," Martin said.

"If you say so."

"You're the one who established the time frame. Maybe it took a few weeks?"

Jill didn't respond. Instead, she glared at both Martin and Pete.

After a protracted wait, Pete resumed the interview. "How is your marriage these days?"

"It's fine. We're doing okay. We're working our way through our problems. It takes time, you know."

"You're able to reach your son, correct?" Pete asked.

"Of course."

"Please do that, and tell him to come home. That way, he'll be here by the time we finish speaking with your daughter."

"Dylan's studying for a class he's struggling with. He has a test tomorrow. It's his final semester. He can't afford to fail the class. If he does, he won't graduate. He works harder for grades than Caitlin. Can't you wait until after the test? He plans to study for at least another two hours. Cutting short this tutoring session could be disastrous. Please, don't do that to Dylan. Wait until tomorrow. *Please.*"

THIRTY-FIVE

Ｉf Dylan isn't home by the time we finish speaking with your daughter, we'll wait until tomorrow. But we'll only do that on the condition that we speak with him before he leaves for school," Martin said. It would mean an early morning for Pete and him, but he was willing to make that concession.

"You can't wait until after school?" Jill pleaded.

"Tonight—or tomorrow morning at six thirty, whichever you prefer," Martin said. His jaw announced there was no room for negotiation.

"Tomorrow, then."

"Okay, now we'll speak with your daughter," Martin said.

After Jill left to get Caitlin, Pete said, "Nice work, Sarge."

Martin's chuckle was barely audible.

Jill returned, followed closely by Caitlin.

Mother and daughter sat across the table from the two investigators. Caitlin looked nervous. Jill looked tired of the intrusion.

"I understand you're quite the student," Martin said.

Caitlin blushed.

"Any ideas what you'd like to do after you finish school?" Martin asked.

The question seemed to energize Caitlin. "Yes, I want to do research. I want to be the one who unlocks the puzzle to curing Alzheimer's."

"That would be wonderful," Martin said. "And it sounds like you have the wherewithal to accomplish it."

"Thanks. I hope so. My grandpa had it. Watching what it did to him was horrible!" Her facial expression drove home her sincerity.

"I hope you succeed. It's a noble effort," Martin said. "Now, I better get down to the reason we're here. We have a few questions for you. You know about the accident on Wheelock Parkway on Tuesday?"

"Yes, how's he doing?"

"He's still unconscious," Martin said.

"Oh. I hope he'll be fine. It's so sad." Caitlin was choked up.

"Sorry to have to ask you this with your mother in the room, but do you sometimes sneak out during the late night or early morning hours?" Martin asked.

"I don't have to sneak out. I've been getting up early for years, off and on, to go running. First I did it because I was on the track and cross country teams. Now I run for endurance and to stay in shape for lacrosse and field hockey."

"You look tired," Martin sympathized. "Have you been getting up early the past several days?"

"No," Caitlin drew it out. "I've had cramps all week." She blushed.

"When you do run in the early morning, what time do you do it?" Martin asked.

"Real early. I have to get home in time to shower and be ready to leave for school by about seven."

"How early?" Martin asked.

"It all depends on how far I'm running."

"And how far do you run at that time of day?" Martin asked.

"It's pretty much the only time I can run, so anywhere from five to eight miles."

"Let's say you're going to run eight miles. When do you have to be out the door to allow time to get home and get ready for school?" Martin asked.

"It depends on how fast I run. If I leave later than I'd planned, I might be out the door as late as five thirty."

"Remind me not to attempt to run with you." Martin smiled. "Then you must not mind early mornings," he continued.

"I'd rather sleep in; but, like I said, it's usually the only chance I have to run."

"How about your brother?" Martin asked. "Is he an early riser?"

"No," she chuckled. "Getting out of bed in time to get to school almost kills him." Her hand shot up, covering her mouth, and her gaze dropped to the table. "Sorry, that's an awful thing to say after what happened to Mr. Rice."

"Guess hating early mornings is pretty normal for a guy Dylan's age, huh?" Martin asked.

Caitlin nodded without looking up.

"Sounds like you and Dylan are pretty close," Martin said.

"Yes. No one has a better brother than Dylan."

"Does Dylan sneak out sometimes?" Martin asked.

"Not that I know of."

"Are you sure?" Martin asked.

Caitlin nodded, concentrating on the tabletop.

"I understand things have been a bit tense around here for the last while," Pete said.

"Yes, but everything's fine now."

"What changed that?" Pete asked.

"The fact the holidays are over, I guess. I'm not really sure." Caitlin shrugged.

"When did you first notice a change?" Pete asked.

"Right after the first of the year or thereabouts, I guess. I'm not sure."

"What was the first thing you noticed that was different?" Pete asked.

"Everyone seemed happier."

"And prior to that?" Pete asked.

Caitlin looked at her mother and asked, "Do I have to tell them, Mom?"

"Yes, you do," Pete interjected.

"Mom and Dad were always fighting. It was so tense any time they were both home."

Jill brought her hand to her mouth, closed her eyes and blushed.

"Did Dylan have a solution for that?" Martin asked.

Caitlin glanced at her mother, then back at the table. "Yes. He told me not to be here when both of them are home."

Jill looked contrite.

"Did Dylan have any other ideas for making things better?" Martin asked.

"No. His solution was to avoid the whole situation."

"Is Dylan a good problem solver?" Pete asked.

"He tries."

"Does he ever help you solve your problems?" Pete asked.

"He's great at sympathizing, but he isn't likely to act."

"People overreact at times," Martin said. "Do you sometimes overreact, Caitlin?"

"I don't think so. Do I, Mom?" Caitlin sounded uncertain.

"No. That doesn't sound like you."

"How about Dylan? Does he ever overreact?" Martin asked.

"No. I don't think so."

"How did he react to the problems between your parents?" Martin asked.

"Like I said, he did everything possible to avoid the problem. When he was here, he spent his time in his room—with his head-phones on and the volume turned up."

"That's all for now, Caitlin," Martin said.

Neither Dylan nor Paul arrived during this questioning.

On their way to the front door, Martin reiterated that he and Pete would return at six thirty the next morning.

Jill again petitioned for a later time, saw it was hopeless, and gave up.

Martin dropped off Pete at headquarters and headed home. He was afraid Marty would be asleep by the time he walked in the door. He hated doing that to his son. Then he realized he'd soon be doing it to his son *and* his daughter.

THIRTY-SIX

Pete and Martin arrived at the Norman residence at six twenty-five in the morning. The sun wouldn't rise for another ninety minutes. It was pitch dark. The streets were quiet. The air had a crispness that was unwelcomed, at least across segments of the Twin Cities population.

Jill answered the door. She appeared ready for work. The look on her face announced her displeasure with the investigators' demands. She led Pete and Martin to the dining room, and instructed them to have a seat. Maintaining the icy tone, she said she'd get Dylan.

Pete and Martin waited for several minutes before Paul walked in.

His face was beet red and looked strained. "We can't find Dylan," he said. He sounded panicky. "He was in his room getting ready for school. I swear, I thought he was still there. I can't imagine where he went."

Pete and Martin were on their feet and putting on their overcoats.

"If you know where he is, you better speak up," Pete said. "Do I need to educate you on the implications and penalties if you don't?"

"I know Dylan isn't responsible for what happened to Nick Rice. I know he was here at the time it happened. I saw him in his bed, sound asleep at six that morning. This is a result of all the stress he's under, thanks to a chemistry test today. I tried to talk him out of taking that class. He might be delaying this meeting while he does another hour of cramming. Please, don't jump to any conclusions."

"The only conclusion I'm jumping to," Martin said, "is that we made a deal with your wife last night. Your son broke the commitment. We intend to find out why. If you know where he is and don't

150

tell us, you could be charged with obstructing an investigation. The question then becomes why you feel compelled to do that."

"I'm not doing that. I swear."

"Is his car here?" Pete asked.

"Yes. I checked a few minutes ago. He couldn't have gone far. I'm sure he'll be right back."

"Did he tell Caitlin she'd have to get a ride with someone else?" Pete asked.

"I don't think so. Caitlin knows we're looking for him. She didn't say anything."

"Get Caitlin," Pete said.

While he and Pete were alone in the dining room, Martin said, "Guess I made a mistake by not forcing Dylan to come home last night."

"No, you did what most fathers would do. His mother gave us a very convincing sales pitch."

When Paul returned with Caitlin, she was crying.

"Where's your brother, Caitlin?" Pete asked.

"I don't know. Honest."

"Are you trying to tell us you didn't see him leave, and he didn't tell you he was going?" Pete was incredulous.

"Yes, that's what I'm saying. It's the truth," she sniffed.

"You're intelligent, and you know your brother. What's your best guess?" Pete asked.

"The only thing I can think of is that he went to a friend's house. He might be getting some last-minute tutoring."

"What's his tutor's name?" Pete asked.

"Logan Clay."

"What's Logan's phone number?" Pete asked.

"I'll get it," Paul said, hurrying out of the dining room.

Caitlin stood in the corner. Her head hung low. She looked devastated.

After Jill joined them, Pete said, "Okay, Caitlin, you know your brother. You can help him by telling us why he took off."

"I don't know," she moaned.

"Leave her alone," Paul protested, returning to the room. "Here's Logan's cell number." He held out a slip of paper for Pete. "I don't think they have a home phone."

"I'll make the call from here," Pete said. "If Dylan isn't with Logan, or if I can't reach Logan, I want a list of all of Dylan's close friends and their parents' names."

After dialing the number, Pete tapped the table with a pen while he waited for Logan to answer. The call went to voicemail.

Seeing the look on Pete's face, Caitlin said, "Logan might not answer if he's busy helping Dylan. He may not want to be interrupted."

Looking at his watch, Pete stood, put on his overcoat and asked, "Does Logan go to Anderson Senior High?"

"Yes," Paul and Caitlin said in unison.

"What time do classes begin?" Pete asked.

"Seven thirty," Paul said, adding, "Let me call some of Dylan's friends. Please, give me a chance to find him."

Pete and Martin sat down.

Paul got a piece of paper. He and Jill compiled a list of Dylan's friends. They split up the calls, working their way through the list, checking off the names as they went. The effort took almost a half-hour.

The stress level in the room became palatable, and the strain on their faces increased as failed attempt built upon failed attempt.

Caitlin offered to help with the calls. Her mother thanked her and said she and Paul would handle it. So Caitlin remained standing in the corner, leaning against the wall, crying.

Jill finished first.

When he disconnected after the last call, Paul threw up his hands in exasperation. "I don't know what else to do. What do you think, Jill?"

She shrugged and shook her head. She looked exhausted.

"We'll take it from here," Pete said. "Does Dylan have a girlfriend?"

"Yes, Ellie Cook," Paul said.

"She's on that list you've been using?" Pete asked, motioning toward the sheet of paper they used to track the friends and parents they contacted.

"Of course," Paul said. "You don't actually believe we're trying to thwart your investigation, do you?"

"Time will tell," Pete said. "I'd like that list or read the names, and I'll make my own."

Paul read the names on the list, while both Pete and Martin made notes. When Paul finished, Pete began at the top and asked for the name of the high school, home address, and phone numbers for each friend and their parents.

"One more question, Caitlin," Pete said. "Who would Dylan go to in an emergency or if he needed help?"

"Logan, definitely Logan. He and Dylan are inseparable. But Dylan isn't in trouble. I know he didn't hurt Mr. Rice," she said with a shaky voice.

"Would he go to Logan rather than his girlfriend?" Pete asked.

"Yes, definitely," Caitlin said.

Her mother nodded in agreement.

Information in hand, the two investigators hurried to the unmarked car.

THIRTY-SEVEN

Before Martin drove anywhere, Pete called Dylan's cell. Prior to a single ring, he was relegated to voicemail. Next he tried Logan Clay's cell. That call was no more successful than his attempt a half-hour ago.

It was seven fifteen. While Martin drove, Pete found the phone numbers for the two high schools that Dylan and his friends attended. School started at seven thirty. They couldn't get to Anderson Senior High, the school Dylan, Logan, and Dylan's girlfriend attended, before then.

He wondered what time the schools began answering the phones, then decided it didn't matter. Face-to-face contacts were preferable.

The Anderson parking lot was full. The only available parking space within blocks of the school would get anyone else a ticket. Martin parked there.

With little effort, they located the office. Several people worked in a bullpen area. A woman saw them, came to the counter, and asked how she could help. Although young, with the exception of slacks, she looked like the stereotypical librarian.

Pete and Martin identified themselves, and Pete explained what they wanted.

The woman spent less than a minute in front of a monitor. Her fingers flew across the keyboard at a speed that mimicked the speed of a hummingbird's wings. She returned and said, "Logan Clay is here. Caitlin and Dylan Norman, and Ellie Cook are not, at least not yet."

"Have their parents called to say they won't be here today?" Pete asked.

"No, not yet."

"Is that unusual?" Pete asked.

"No. Since it isn't eight o'clock, we may still get a call from their parents. Also, lots of times parents don't call. Instead, the student brings a note when they return."

"Do the same parents usually send a note rather than call?" Pete asked.

"No, it varies."

"We want to talk to Logan Clay," Pete said. "Should I ask you or someone else to pull him out of class?"

"I'll get him for you. It will only take a few minutes. When I return, I'll set you up in an office. I assume you want privacy."

Pete nodded and thanked her.

True to her word, the woman returned shortly. A big kid, presumably Logan Clay, walked alongside her.

Pete estimated the boy's height as six feet and his weight as 200 pounds. He was anything but fat. He had huge shoulders and forearms.

Pete couldn't help wondering if the boy used steroids. The drugs were a sad commentary on the short-sighted priorities of some young people and adults.

Logan's hair was dark brown and looked uncombed. His gray eyes were penetrating. He wore a baggy jersey, and jeans that fit somewhat, possibly due to the school's policy prohibiting saggy pants.

The woman told Logan these were the men who wanted to see him, and Logan shook hands with each man, saying, "Logan Clay, sir."

Pete and Martin introduced themselves and showed Logan their badges and IDs.

Logan rolled his shoulders. He looked nervous.

The office employee led Pete, Martin, and Logan to a compact room in the back corner. The room felt sterile. A desk and chair sat on the far end. Three chairs faced the desk. Pete thought it unlikely this room was used much for conveying good news. How many parents had their dreams dashed here or in a room like it?

The woman said they could use the office as long as they needed it.

"Have a seat," Pete told Logan, after she left.

He and Martin selected chairs once Logan did so. They moved in close, complicating an early exit by the young man.

"How old are you?" Pete asked.

"Eighteen, sir."

"Have you spoken with Dylan Norman this morning?" Martin asked.

"Yes. Why?"

"What time?" Martin asked.

"Around six."

"He called your cell?" Martin asked.

"Yes, sir."

"In the last hour, I called you twice," Pete said. "You didn't answer either time."

Logan shrugged.

"I think it's because Dylan told you the police might call and asked you not to answer," Pete said.

"No sir! I'm almost out of minutes for the month. I'm not answering anytime I don't know who it is."

"Where's Dylan?" Martin asked.

"Don't know."

"Is he in school today?" Pete asked.

"Don't know that, either. Never see him this early."

"What did you talk about when he called?" Pete asked.

"He was upset about the cops coming to his house."

"Why?" Pete asked.

"Isn't that normal?"

"What else did you talk about?" Pete asked.

"That's all."

"Did he ask you to skip school with him today?" Pete asked.

"Well, yeah."

"And?" Pete asked.

"I said I couldn't. My team has a presentation today."

"Is Dylan on that team?" Pete asked.

"No, sir."

"Where did he plan to go?" Pete asked.

"Don't know. He didn't say."

Pete told Logan that concealing information could result in charges of obstruction.

"I wouldn't do that, sir. I want to go to Notre Dame. My parents don't have that kind of money. I can't swing it unless I get a scholarship. I've dreamt of going there since I was like four years old. I applied. I'll hear back in April. I won't do anything to screw it up."

Pete jumped on this tangent. "Anything like what Dylan asked you to do, right?"

"No, sir. He didn't ask me to do anything that could get me in trouble. He knows how I feel about Notre Dame. He wouldn't do anything to ruin it for me. In fact, he keeps saying he can't wait to spend a weekend there with me."

"Caitlin said he's been very unhappy about the atmosphere around their house," Pete said.

"I guess. Wouldn't you be, if you were him?"

"I hear he came up with a creative way to solve the problem," Pete said.

"Yes, sir. Dylan's been at my house more than his. I don't mind. Neither do my parents. He's quiet and polite, and he's good to hang with."

"What did he tell you about the accident on Wheelock Parkway on Tuesday?" Pete asked.

"You mean the one where Mr. Rice was hit by a car?"

"Yes," Pete said.

"All he said was that the guy was the husband of his dad's old girlfriend."

"I'll bet, in light of the circumstances, that he thought the accident was a form of retribution, right?" Pete asked.

"No. He said he couldn't believe the guy got knocked down twice."

"What did he mean by that?" Pete asked.

"He knew how angry his mom was with his dad. He figured Mr. Rice had to be just as angry. Maybe even more so. It had to be a blow to his ego! Then, to make things worse, he got hit by a car. That was the second time."

"So Dylan believes Rice was hit intentionally," Pete said.

"I don't know. He didn't say that."

It took several repetitions and a great deal of patience to learn that Dylan's favorite escape was the family's cabin near the Boundary Waters Canoe Area. There were places Logan thought he might go around the Twin Cities, but not in the winter. He also said he knew Dylan wouldn't go to the Boundary Waters by himself. He was sure Dylan would show up that day.

"And you're basing that on?" Martin asked.

"Dylan needs to be around people. He doesn't like to be alone."

"Maybe he took his girlfriend with him," Martin suggested.

"I doubt it. Her parents would kill both of them."

"What's his girlfriend's name?" Martin asked.

"Ellie Cook."

"Let's talk hypothetically," Pete said. "To whom would Dylan go if he needed help and, say, you were at Notre Dame?"

"I think he'd come to Notre Dame." Logan smiled.

"Suppose he couldn't get there. Then what?" Pete asked.

Logan added a few names to the list provided by Paul and Jill Norman, then said, "But I don't think he's with any of them."

"Why's that?" Pete asked.

"I don't know." Logan shrugged. "I just don't think he is."

"Has Dylan been angry or irritable ever since the first of the year?" Pete asked.

"No."

"But he's more tired these days, isn't he." Pete said.

"No. He's the same as always."

"But he was a wreck on Tuesday, the day Rice was struck, wasn't he?" Pete asked.

"He's been a wreck since last weekend. He's afraid he'll flunk the chemistry exam."

"I think Dylan had something to do with what happened to Rice," Pete said. "That would explain his disappearance."

"I know Dylan, and I know you're wrong."

"Then why did he take off before we could speak with him? Looks mighty suspicious, wouldn't you say, Logan?" Pete asked.

"No, sir. Not necessarily."

"Why are you so nervous?" Pete asked.

"Wouldn't you be if you were being grilled by the police?" Logan used a sleeve to wipe sweat from his forehead.

"Do we need to revisit the whole obstruction issue?" Pete asked.

"No, sir, I'm telling the truth."

"I suggest you call or text Dylan, and tell him to give me a call. Here's my card," Pete said, handing one to Logan.

Logan took it and said he'd do what he could, but he doubted Dylan had his phone turned on.

When Pete, Martin, and Logan emerged from the office, the woman who'd helped the two investigators had a message for them. Ellie Cook's mother called. Ellie was home, sick.

On their way to the second school, Pete spoke with Ellie Cook and her mother. He started with the mother, verifying that she wasn't covering for Dylan and her daughter. Then he told her it was important she notify him immediately, if she or her daughter heard from Dylan. She didn't ask for an explanation.

Ellie told him that Dylan called and asked if she knew where he could hang for a few days. She didn't, and he hung up before answering her questions. She was furious about that.

Pete hoped that increased the likelihood she'd notify him, if Dylan called again. It would help to know if Dylan was a skilled peacemaker.

THIRTY-EIGHT

P ete called the office at Warren Senior High and requested the status of the four students he and Martin wanted to interview.

A staff member checked and only two of the four were in school. The other two were out sick. Both had an excused absence. In both cases, a parent called that morning.

Three of Dylan's best friends were out sick. Sounded suspicious. Pete asked if the absentee rate was that high throughout the school.

"A virus has been making its way through Warren. If a student is sick, we hope they stay home to prevent spreading it. Often, that doesn't happen. Today's absentee rate is nowhere near fifty percent, but I don't have detailed data. However, it is common for a virus to hit a group of friends simultaneously," she explained.

For the remainder of the trip, Pete was on the phone with the parents of the two ill Warren students.

Despite the potential implications he outlined, both parents confirmed that their daughters were home ill. Neither girl answered her cell when Pete called.

At Warren, Pete and Martin started with Noah Wilkin. Logan Clay provided his name. Noah was small and studious-looking, with straight brown hair and cowlicks at both temples. His blue eyes looked at them worriedly, through black-framed glasses.

"What time did Dylan call you this morning?" Martin asked.

"Dylan doesn't call that often, unless a bunch of us are getting together."

"How old are you, Noah?" Martin asked.

"Eighteen." Noah assumed an upright stance and authoritative expression.

"Perfect," Martin said. "We'll take you to headquarters and question you there. Get your jacket and..."

"A little after six."

"What did he want?" Martin asked.

"He wanted me to take him to my cousin's apartment."

"Where is that apartment?" Martin asked.

"In Hudson. You know, Wisconsin?"

"Yeah, I've heard of it," Martin said, concealing a smile. "What did you tell Dylan?"

"I like Dylan, but I know he called me because Logan wouldn't help. I don't know why he wanted to hang at my cousin's."

"How long did he want to stay there?" Martin asked.

"He said a week or more. I don't want to spend a week sleeping on the floor at my cousin's, especially when Logan would probably show up and spend a lot of time there, too."

"How old is your cousin?" Martin asked.

"Nineteen. He graduated last year."

"What did Dylan say after you ruled out Wisconsin?" Martin asked.

"He made me promise I wouldn't tell anyone that he asked." Noah bit his lower lip, and jammed his hands in his pockets.

"Not a problem," Martin said. "Get your jacket. We'll figure it out at headquarters."

"Okay, okay. Then he wanted to know if he could stay at my house."

"And?" Martin asked.

"I told him my dad's on vacation, so I'd never get away with it."

"Get away with what?" Martin asked.

"With having him there all day while I'm in school. It would be one thing if he was going to school, too."

"Why is he going to skip school?" Martin asked.

"I don't know. He didn't say."

Martin gave him a "yeah, sure" look.

"Seriously, he didn't tell me."

"And you didn't think to ask?" Martin persisted.

"I asked. He said he had to go."

"Go where?" Martin asked.

"He didn't mean it that way." Noah looked exasperated.

"Before you go, I want to make sure you understand what will happen if you know where Dylan is and refuse to tell us," Martin said.

"Yeah, I've heard."

"Okay. Just remember, there are nicer places to work on your GED," Martin said.

"I know. I know. I'm telling the truth!" Noah screamed.

THIRTY-NINE

Just think, Martin, your son is well on his way to being just like the boys who've helped us so far. Makes you want to speed up the clock, doesn't it?"

"Or freeze Marty at age ten. Tell me again, Pete, why do you want to have kids?"

"Because I have masochistic tendencies?"

"Really? I think Logan would peg you as a sadist."

"But, Martin, think what I'd be like if I detested kids."

"That's scary. Do you think Dylan was really that secretive? Or are these kids bent on protecting him?"

"Could go either way, Martin. Is three your lucky number? Here comes the third and final healthy person on our list of friends."

Justin Todd looked like he'd been deposited in St. Paul by a large wave. His hair was long, blond, and disheveled. He either had olive-colored skin or spent a portion of each week in a tanning booth. His blue eyes and blond eyebrows added credence to the color of his hair.

Justin wore a broad smile as he approached Pete and Martin. Pete didn't think anyone called to the school office would walk in wearing a smile. At least not when he was a kid.

Pete told Justin to have a seat. During the preliminaries, he got Justin's address and cell and home numbers. He learned that after school and on weekends Justin worked at the Cambridge Garden Center, the same nursery where Kevin Douglas worked. When he asked about Kevin, Justin said he was a nice guy who never seemed to catch a break.

"How long have you known Dylan Norman?" Pete asked.

"Forever. We went to grade school together."

"A guy would go a long way to help someone he'd known as long as you've known Dylan, wouldn't he," Pete said.

"Depends on the friend."

"I'd guess that Dylan is that kind of friend," Pete said.

"Depends." Justin looked stoic.

"Depends on?" Pete asked.

"The kind of help needed."

"Dylan called you this morning, didn't he?" Pete said.

"No. It's a school day."

"How old are you, Justin?" Pete asked.

"Eighteen."

"What do you say, Martin? Will we get some straight answers if we let him spend the night in jail, and talk to him tomorrow? We don't have time to hang around here, waiting on him."

"Good idea," Martin said. He stood and put on his overcoat.

Pete stood and stepped to Justin's side. "Stand up, son," he said.

"Okay, fine. Yes, Dylan called this morning."

"What did he want?" Pete asked.

"He wanted me to go up north with him."

"Where up north?" Martin asked.

"The Boundary Waters."

"What did he plan to do there?" Martin asked.

"Hang."

"For how long?" Martin asked.

"I don't know. I said I couldn't go, so he didn't say."

"What time did he call?" Martin asked.

"Six fifteen or so. He woke me up."

"And you weren't the first one he called, were you?" Martin asked.

"No."

"Who else did he call?" Martin asked.

"Logan and Noah."

"What did he ask them?" Martin asked.

"Like I said, he wanted to go up north."

"What else did he want?" Martin asked.

"He wanted us to take my car."

"Why your car?" Pete asked.

"I didn't ask."

"He has a car. Why not take his car?" Pete asked.

"I don't know!"

"What kind of car do you drive?" Pete asked.

"A Taurus."

"What year?" Pete asked.

"2002."

"And the color?" Pete asked.

"White."

"Dylan told you about the problems with his parents, didn't he?" Pete said.

"Yeah."

"Was he angry about it?" Pete asked.

"He didn't like it, but Caitlin's the one who freaked."

"So you talked to Caitlin about it," Pete said.

"Yeah."

"What did you say?" Pete asked.

"I told her, 'Been there, done that. Get over it.' I said she isn't the first, and won't be the last person, to deal with it."

"How did she react?" Pete asked.

"For like a month, every time I saw her, she ignored me."

"Then?" Pete asked.

"She got over it, and everything was cool."

"Did Dylan hear what you told Caitlin?" Pete asked.

"Yeah. I only see her when I'm with him."

"How did he react to what you told her?" Pete asked.

"He was furious."

"Sounds like Dylan takes care of his little sister," Martin said.

"For sure." Justin nodded.

"And Dylan wanted to fix the problem upsetting Caitlin," Martin said.

"Of course. Do you have a sister?" Momentarily, Justin slipped from stoic to a *well, duh* expression.

"How did he do that?"

"Do what?"

"Fix things for Caitlin," Pete said.

"I didn't say he did, only that he wanted to. There was no way he could fix it."

"What did Dylan say when you refused to help him?" Pete asked.

"Like I said, he was pretty angry."

"I'll bet he was more than angry. I'll bet he exploded," Pete said. Then, to force a response, he went into a holding pattern.

Eventually, Justin sighed and said, "Yeah."

"What did he blurt out when he exploded?" Pete asked.

"He said he didn't need me anyway."

"Since you didn't help, where was he going next?" Pete asked.

"He didn't say."

"I'll bet you know Dylan almost as well as he knows himself," Pete said.

"If you say so."

"You know the family members he's closest to, don't you, Justin?" Pete said.

"No."

Pete looked at his watch and said, "We're in a hurry."

Justin smiled.

"Get your jacket, Justin. You're coming with us. Martin, I need your cuffs." Pete held out a hand.

"His grandma or his dad's sister," Justin blurted out. "They're the only ones he'd go to."

"I need names and addresses," Pete said.

Justin knew the aunt's first name, but not her married name. He didn't have addresses, but he provided roundabout directions to the two homes.

In parting, Pete said, "If you're lying, Justin, we're coming after you. That isn't a threat. It's a fact."

Before leaving Warren Senior High, Pete and Martin checked Noah's and Justin's attendance records for Tuesday—three days ago.

FORTY

Dylan had a special connection with a grandmother and an aunt. Thankfully, both of their homes were more accessible than the family's cabin near the Boundary Waters.

Pete remembered seeking refuge with his grandparents, after getting into scrapes at home. They had a special knack for sympathizing, without taking his side. He never doubted that they loved him and would do anything in their power to help him.

For that reason, finding Dylan at his grandmother's seemed reasonable. If Dylan wasn't there, the aunt was next on their list. Would those family members help or hinder their investigation?

Along those lines, was Jill lying to Martin and him last night? If Dylan had a critical test today, it didn't stop him from skipping school.

Jill and Paul Norman seemed genuinely upset about Dylan's disappearance. Were they skilled actors? Had their marriage necessitated the development and fine-tuning of those skills?

If Dylan was with a grandmother or an aunt, what could he and Martin expect from those family members? No sense looking at his own family. Thus far, the disparities between his family and Dylan's were too great to provide a hint.

In all likelihood, the grandmother or aunt would believe what Dylan told them. If Dylan was with one of them, he was probably counting on it. That could prove to be a problem.

Pete wondered if Dylan snuck home and got his car, after he and Martin left. Would he think it through, realizing driving his car painted a bull's-eye on his back? Seemed he knew that, since he left without it this morning. Add to that his attempts to use a friend's car for his escape. Even so...

Pete had a squad dispatched to the Norman home. Another thought. Did Paul and Jill give Dylan a credit card for gasoline? If so, whether or not Dylan had his car, any activity on the card could help locate the boy.

Judging from one of Justin's comments and Dylan's desperate attempts to find someone to disappear with, he wasn't much of a loner. His three "best" male friends failed him. Would he ask one of the girls? Even more important, if he drove the vehicle that hit Rice, did he do that alone or recruit an accomplice?

While he and Martin traveled the twenty miles to Hugo, Pete contacted the mothers of the three absent students a second time. Ellie's mother was home the first time he spoke with her. Now all three girls were home alone. Pete explained that he needed more than an assurance their daughters were home ill. He told the three mothers to have their daughters call him ASAP.

Two of the three called immediately. Both heard from a frantic Dylan that morning, between six fifteen and six thirty. The girls said they told him they were too sick to go anywhere. Dylan was exasperated. He told both that they couldn't possibly be that sick. He claimed if the situation was reversed, he would drop everything to help them. He said he might call again. He didn't.

Finally, both girls relented and promised to call Pete immediately if Dylan called again.

Pete assured each girl that the best thing they could do for Dylan was to get him to call either him or Martin.

While speaking with the girls, he got a text message. Dylan's Camry was still parked on the street in front of the Norman home.

During the remainder of the trip to Hugo, the two investigators conferred over how to proceed. They decided they had no choice when it came to the next step.

FORTY-ONE

Pete and Martin passed a new and upscale section of Hugo. A devastating tornado struck that neighborhood in the spring of 2008, leaving death and destruction in its wake. Demolished homes were rebuilt, and the disaster had no discernible effect on subsequent construction. Now, only a handful of vacant lots remained.

Jill Norman's mother lived roughly three miles away, in the center of Hugo. The large, ranch-style house was built in the seventies and occupied a corner lot. There was a stand of huge pines just inside the backyard fence.

The investigators got out of the unmarked and went in different directions.

Pete checked through the windows of the car parked in the driveway. Then he stood watch in the front yard, where he had an unobstructed view of the front door and the overhead door of the attached garage. He hoped he wouldn't be forced into a footrace with Dylan.

Meanwhile, Martin inspected the other three sides of the house, looking for all possible exits. He identified four likely options. The first was a sliding glass door into the dining room. There were two egress windows in the basement, and a door into the garage. All four of those exits placed an escapee in the fenced backyard. A kid who ran the hurdles could clear that four-foot fence. Martin shook his head. He knew someone as fast as Dylan would be in the next county by the time he was on the other side of the fence.

After he described his findings, Pete ascended the four steps to the front door. He rang the doorbell and stepped back, keeping an eye on the garage and the front yard.

A tall, slender woman answered the door. She had green eyes and a deeply wrinkled face. Jill looked like a younger version of this woman.

"May I help you?" she asked.

"I'm looking for your grandson, Dylan Norman," Pete said, displaying his badge and ID. "I know he's here."

"Please, come in."

"Sorry, ma'am, he'll have to come to the door."

"But I'd like to speak with you before you talk to Dylan," the woman pleaded. She looked on the verge of tears.

"That isn't possible. We've been chasing your grandson since six thirty this morning. I'm willing to listen to you, but only after your grandson is in our car."

"Do you have to do that? I mean..."

"Ma'am, I'm not willing to discuss it before I see Dylan."

"I can't believe..."

"You leave me no choice. I'll call for backup," Pete said, and pulled the cell from his pocket.

"No, please, don't. I'll get him. Come in."

"No, ma'am. I'll wait here."

When she returned, Dylan was at her side.

Pete compared the boy to a photo he saw in the Norman home. This kid wasn't the carefree, happy person in that picture. He looked like he hadn't slept in days. His cheeks were hollow, and his face looked gray. His shoulders slumped. His eyes were fixated on his toes.

Pete speed-dialed Martin, on the cell he still held.

"Dylan, we're taking you to headquarters for questioning," Pete said.

"Ma'am, please get his things. While you do, he'll stay here with me." Pete's tone left no room for discussion.

Dylan looked at his grandmother. The despondent, pleading look gave Pete and Martin, who now stood at Pete's side, a glimpse into the relationship between grandmother and grandson.

Pete steeled himself. He couldn't let it influence him.

Dylan's grandmother returned, carrying a jacket. After Dylan shrugged into it, she hugged him tightly for several seconds.

Pete saw her whisper something into Dylan's ear. He couldn't hear what.

As much as he would like to forego the handcuffs, Pete couldn't trust the kid.

When the boy was handcuffed, Pete and Martin each grasped one of his arms and escorted him to the unmarked.

Pete put a hand on the top of Dylan's head, guiding him into the backseat.

Dylan didn't resist.

Riding in the unmarked saved him the embarrassment of making the trip in a squad, but Pete figured that probably never occurred to Dylan anyway. How the kid got downtown was insignificant, compared to the issues he now faced.

FORTY-TWO

Martin stayed with Dylan, while Pete returned to the boy's grandmother.

She stood jacketless on the front steps, tears flowing.

"I promised to hear you out, ma'am. What do you want to tell me?"

"May I come with you?"

"Not in the department's car, ma'am."

"Where are you taking Dylan? Will I be able to see him?"

"We're taking him to headquarters. You can see him, but it might be hours. I suggest you wait here."

She demanded the address, and Pete provided it.

"Dylan is the sweetest boy I know. He isn't the person you're looking for."

"Who is that person?"

"I don't know," she wept. "He wouldn't tell me. Surely Jill and Paul know he didn't do it. Didn't you talk to them?"

"Sorry, ma'am. I can't discuss it."

"I don't understand why you're doing this. It's criminal!"

Pete returned to the unmarked. This time, he drove while Martin rode in the backseat with Dylan. If Dylan so much as opened his mouth on the way to headquarters, Pete would Mirandize him.

Dylan's head hung low. His eyes were closed. His fists were clenched.

Driving to headquarters, Pete saw Dylan's grandmother in the rearview mirror. She must have grabbed a coat and been out the door, almost on his heels.

Reaching headquarters, Pete and Martin took Dylan to Homicide and put him in an interview room.

Pete recited the date and location, then told Dylan to state his name and age.

Video and audio taping equipment captured everything.

"I'm Dylan Norman. I'm eighteen."

Pete immediately Mirandized Dylan, reading the words in a clear voice and measured pace.

Dylan said he understood, and he didn't want an attorney.

"Are you sure you don't want an attorney, Dylan?" Pete asked.

"I'm positive," Dylan mumbled. He looked dazed.

"I like to run in the early morning, Dylan," Pete said. "I like having time to myself. I could probably be happy spending my life on a deserted island. How about you, Dylan?"

"No way!"

"I hear you ran the forty in 4.32. For real?" Pete asked.

Dylan blushed and gave a hesitant half-smile. "Guess my dad told you, huh?"

"Yes, and if you were my kid, I'd tell everyone who would listen—at least once."

Dylan smiled. "Thanks. It took a lot of hard work."

"I'm sure it did. I think heredity can also play a part. Caitlin's a runner, too. Do you run with Caitlin?" Pete asked.

"Rarely."

"Do your parents run?" Pete asked.

"Sometimes. Not often."

"Are they fast?"

"They'll never set any records, but they do okay." Dylan shrugged.

"Your speed came in handy last Tuesday, didn't it," Pete said.

Dylan stared at his hands and didn't answer.

"I hear you're very protective of Caitlin," Pete said.

Hands up shrug.

"When we couldn't find you, we talked to Logan," Pete said.

Dylan clenched his fists.

"It's a shame Notre Dame will no longer be able to accept him," Pete said.

"Logan didn't do anything," Dylan muttered.

"We also spoke with Noah," Pete said.

Silence.

"Why Nicholas Rice, Dylan? What did he do to deserve this?"

Dylan's shoulders tightened. "You wouldn't understand."

"Understand what?" Pete asked.

Dylan stared at his clasped hands. He didn't answer.

"Help me understand, Dylan," Pete said. "I want to understand. Nicholas Rice's kids want to understand."

Dylan continued staring silently at his hands.

"Revenge is sweet, isn't it, Dylan?" Pete probed. "There's a special kind of satisfaction at the moment the axe drops. Seeing Nicholas Rice's face as the car slammed him into that tree must have given you an unbeatable high. I'll bet it was priceless, wasn't it, Dylan? Where will you get your next high?"

Dylan closed his eyes and bit his lower lip.

"What was Rice wearing when you struck him?" Pete asked.

"Black sweats."

"You had help, didn't you, Dylan. Who helped you?" Pete asked.

Dylan's still closed eyes blinked, once.

"Who drove, Dylan, you or your accomplice? If you tell us who else was involved, we could cut a deal." Pete said.

"I didn't have any help."

"Your sentence could be reduced to..."

"I didn't have any help. I did it. Just me."

"Where did you get the car?" Pete asked.

"From a guy who works with a couple of my friends."

"What's the guy's name?" Pete asked.

Silence.

"What was the make and model of the car you used?" Martin asked.

"A Buick LeSabre."

"Why didn't you use your car, Dylan?" Martin asked.

Silence.

"Why did you want to kill Nicholas Rice?" Martin asked.

"I didn't intend to kill him. I only wanted to hurt him."

"Why did you want to hurt him?" Martin asked.

Silence.

"What were you wearing on Tuesday, when you went after Rice?" Martin asked.

Dylan rested his elbows on his knees, put his hands over his ears, and stared at the floor.

"How did you know the person you went after was Rice?" Martin asked.

Dylan didn't speak or change his position, but both investigators knew he heard the question.

"Okay, I'll give you one more chance," Martin said. "How did you select the spot where you attacked Rice?"

Dylan didn't move, and there was no discernible reaction.

"You know, Dylan, I'd have pegged you as a better driver. I'd have thought you could do a better job of whatever it was you planned to do to Nicholas Rice. Hell, I bet Caitlin could have done a better job, and she's only sixteen." Pete frowned when this attempt to get a reaction failed.

"How did you decide what way to get even?" Pete asked.

"I've said all I'm going to."

"If you want us to believe you, you have to give us more information," Pete said.

"I don't believe that."

"We know you didn't do it alone, Dylan. Who helped you?" Pete asked.

Silence.

"Nicholas Rice has a young family, Dylan," Pete said. "His kids are suffering. How would you feel if someone murdered your dad when you were eight years old? How about doing something for those three little kids?"

Tears dripped on Dylan's lap. He refused to meet Pete's gaze.

"Ever let someone take the rap for you, Dylan?" Pete asked. "If so, you know how it feels. You know the guilt eats away at you. It's one thing if you don't care about the person who takes the rap. It's awful if you care. And the higher the price the other person pays for you, the harder it is to cope. Anyone with a conscience eventually crumbles. Sometimes it ends in suicide. It's a living hell. You know someone who is about to be thrown into that torture chamber, don't you, Dylan. Will you throw them a lifeline or just let them drown?"

"I told you. I did it. Just me." Dylan's voice was robotic.

Pete wondered if he sought to avoid disclosing anything by masking all expression in his voice.

"Your inability to answer my questions indicates you don't have the answers," Pete said.

"I did it. You can't force me to say anything else!"

"Any idea what your sentence will be, Dylan?" Pete asked. "You arranged for a car in advance. That's premeditation. Nicholas Rice's future is doubtful. If he dies, you'll get life. How will it feel when your parents, Caitlin, and Logan visit you in prison? Never mind. They may not bother—at least not after the first time. It isn't a fun place to visit. It's an even worse place to live. Think about it. Every holiday—prison. If Caitlin or your mother need you? Sorry, you're behind bars—forever."

"You know, Commander, Caitlin could take the rap for her big brother. She's only sixteen. She'd only go to juvenile detention. Her record would be expunged in a few years. Tempting as it might be, guess she doesn't want the guilt to eat Dylan alive."

"True, Sergeant. Besides, Dylan loves his sister too much to let her do that for him. He's not that selfish."

Silence.

"You're eighteen, Dylan," Pete said. "Your whole life is ahead of you. You'll end up in Stillwater or worse. You have no idea what it's like. By the time you find out, it'll be too late. You're in a tough spot, and I'd like to help you. But I can't help you if you won't help yourself. We need details. Answer our questions, and we'll cut a deal. This is a one-time offer. You have five minutes to decide if you're going to help yourself and us. After that, the offer is off the table. Are you clear on that, Dylan?"

Ears still covered, Dylan nodded.

Pete and Martin walked out.

Dylan was left alone to decide his fate.

FORTY-THREE

An investigator corralled Pete and Martin as the interview room door closed behind them. "The father's here with an attorney," she said. "They arrived about fifteen minutes after you. He demanded to see his son before he was questioned. He swears you'll be walking a beat by the time he's through with you, Commander. I hope you have some good walking shoes. You'll probably be able to give up running. You'll be walking more than five miles a day while on duty." She grinned.

"Thanks for the sympathy, Brittany."

"Do you want to talk to the father now?" she asked.

"Don't have time. We gave the kid five minutes. I'd hate to keep him waiting."

"I'll bet," she chuckled, nodding.

"Nice speech, to the kid I mean," Martin said when they reached Pete's office. "I almost said I was his accomplice." Martin wasn't smiling.

The two investigators discussed Dylan's refusal to answer questions and some of his reactions. "We have to get at the parts of the story he's hiding. If he still won't talk, once he's booked, we'll meet with the friends we haven't yet seen face to face, then go back to his family and other friends, as needed," Pete said. "The answers are out there, we just have to get at them."

"Just? Are you anticipating a cakewalk?"

"Anything but."

"How does a kid like that get himself into such a fix?" Martin asked.

"Or, who is he willing to sacrifice his life to protect, and why?"

"That's the million-dollar question. Do you think he'll take you up on your offer, Pete?"

"Unfortunately, no. I'll be surprised if he does."

Pete was right. When he and Martin returned to the interview room, Dylan's silence persisted. He didn't utter a word.

While Martin stayed in the interview room with Dylan, Pete went to find a uniformed officer.

Dylan was jailed. Ordinarily they'd have thirty-six hours to either file charges or release him. It was Friday afternoon. They'd bought some extra time.

Pete knew they didn't have enough to charge, much less convict him. They had a lot to accomplish in a few days.

First, however, they had to deal with the wrath of Paul V. Norman.

FORTY-FOUR

Pete and Martin listened to Paul Norman's ranting for two or three minutes. Then Pete interrupted him. "Your son was Mirandized before he said anything other than his name and age. He was given the opportunity to have an attorney present. He decided against it. He's eighteen. He has every right to make that decision. He confessed. Now he's in jail."

"You coerced him. I know he didn't do it!"

"Then who did?" Pete asked.

Norman did an imitation of his son. He didn't respond.

"That's what I thought. You're trying to protect your son."

"I'm telling you, I can prove he's innocent."

"Then I suggest you do that. Regarding coercion, like I said, the interview was recorded." Pete turned and walked away.

Martin was at his side.

After they were out of earshot, Martin tried to lighten the mood. "Two award-winning speeches in one day. Is that some kind of record?"

"I think the record is three. That's why the next one will be up to you." Pete smiled. "You know, Martin, Dylan isn't interested in working a deal. It would help if we knew why."

"Maybe he doesn't trust us. Wouldn't that be novel?"

"True, but if he has nothing to lose..."

"Or if he thinks we'll never be able to prove it anyway."

"Good point, Martin. If that's the reason, wouldn't he want a lawyer? He has to know his dad would get the best that money can buy. In his dad's opinion, Dylan's a rock star kid."

Pete and Martin met with the senior commander of Homicide and Robbery. They discussed the status of their investigation, and the need and justification for a search warrant. They wanted to know with whom Dylan conferred. His cell should, minimally, tell part of that story.

Commander Lincoln decided to conduct a meeting. At that meeting, he brought all available homicide investigators up to speed on the case and assigned the preparation of the search warrant to a member of the staff. It would take about an hour. It would take another hour or a little longer to get it signed by a judge.

Once they had the warrant, the forensics people in the unit would get Dylan's phone from the bag that contained his possessions. They would access recent calls and contact the service provider to get months' worth of information.

For the sake of expediency, while that process was underway, Pete and Martin continued where they left off.

Previously, through parents, Pete instructed Dylan's three sick friends to call him. Two of the three had done so. They decided to start with the third of these friends—Dylan's girlfriend, Ellie Cook.

Pete began with Ellie's mother. She was surprised that her daughter hadn't called. She said she'd get right back to Pete.

Five minutes later, she did. Her daughter wasn't answering, so she resorted to the home phone. The not-so-pretty details were that Ellie rushed into the bathroom, feeling she was about to throw up. She put her phone on the counter next to the toilet. She felt dizzy. Grabbing the counter to stand, she knocked the phone into the toilet.

Ellie dialed Pete's number before she ran to the bathroom. She did everything but press the talk button. After the phone fell in the toilet, she didn't have Pete's phone number. She didn't care. She was too upset about the ruined phone.

She never thought about calling her mother to get Pete's number. She collapsed into bed and fell asleep.

Ellie was still hoping the phone would dry out, and she'd be able to salvage it. She was already on her second phone since school began, and wasn't likely to get another.

"Do you by any chance have a daughter?" Ellie's mother asked. "If you do, you know this is perfectly normal for a teenage girl."

Pete relayed the story to Martin, beginning to end. "Better prepare yourself, Martin, in just over thirteen years you'll have your very own teenage girl," Pete laughed.

Martin laughed, too. "Yeah, and tell me one more time why you still want to have kids?"

Despite the threat of exposure to whatever, Pete and Martin went to the Cook home for a meeting with Ellie.

She was Dylan's girlfriend, and Pete wondered how much Dylan shared with her. How much of it would Ellie share with them?

"Maybe she can narrow the explanations for Dylan's behavior," Pete told Martin. "If not, we'll make our way through the people Dylan might confide in."

Ellie answered the door, dressed in baggy gray sweatpants and an oversized gray hoodie. She was petite and fine-featured with a button nose and tiny ears. She didn't look sick.

Giving her the benefit of the doubt, Pete thought that spending half the day in bed might have helped.

Ellie invited them in, and they sat in the living room.

Pete began by telling her, "I understand Dylan was angry with a guy named Nicholas Rice. Did he talk to you about it?"

"No." She drew it out for a good five seconds. Dylan could have run eighty yards in the time it took her to say that word.

"No, but... ?" Pete asked.

"But he would *never* hurt the guy."

"Unless?" Pete asked.

"Unless nothing." A shake of her head emphasized Ellie's response.

"But he might do it for someone else," Pete said.

"I don't think so."

"I understand life has been tense around his home for a while," Martin said.

"True." She nodded.

"Was Dylan angry about it?" Martin asked.

"Not angry. Just unhappy that his dad would hurt his mom that way."

"His mother was pretty angry?" Martin asked.

"Wouldn't you be?"

"Maybe Dylan wanted to get even for his mother's sake," Martin said.

"By hurting the woman's husband? That would be pretty stupid."

"Is Dylan close to his mother?" Martin asked.

"Yes, very. I sometimes tease him about being a mama's boy."

"I'll bet he loves that," Martin said.

"He knows I'm teasing."

"Are Dylan and Caitlin close?"

"Very. You'd think he was her mother."

"How was Caitlin dealing with the situation around their home the last several months?" Martin asked.

"Not well. She was pretty upset over the whole thing."

"Upset and angry?" Martin asked.

"I suppose she was angry with her dad. I'd be angry with him if he was my dad."

"Dylan and Logan are pretty close?" Martin asked.

"He spends a lot more time with Logan than with me, if that's what you mean."

"How has Logan been the last several weeks?" Pete asked.

"First nervous, then upset. Are you almost finished? I want to go back to bed."

"Getting close," Pete said. "What's Logan been nervous about?"

"About getting into Notre Dame." Ellie smiled.

"And what was he angry about?" Pete asked.

"About not getting into Notre Dame."

"Who told you that?" Pete asked.

"Sydney Brown."

FORTY-FIVE

What are your thoughts on moving Sydney Brown to the top of our list?" Pete asked after they walked out of Ellie's home.

"Seems logical but, using the laws of probability, so does talking to Logan, Caitlin, and Jill Norman."

"Wow, which law of probability would that be?" Pete asked.

"You use it all the time when you decide the information you've gathered about a person of interest excludes them from further investigation. Sometimes we don't have enough information to exclude the person. We move along with the option of returning to that person, until we know the person and the event are mutually exclusive."

"Martin, are you sure your name isn't Charlie Eppes?"

"I thought you didn't watch cop shows on TV. How do you know about the characters in *NUMB3RS*?"

"I used to watch it. I was fascinated by the way Charlie used algorithms to help his FBI brother solve crimes. It's still on cable. Anyway, Martin, can you think of anything that excludes any of the people we're still considering?"

"Unfortunately, no."

"In other words," Pete said, "stay the course."

"Precisely, my dear Watson."

"Did your matrix tell you that?"

"No, but one of the things it can indicate, and should help decipher, is when the crime and a person of interest are mutually exclusive."

Martin stopped four houses down the street from Sydney's.

The investigators wondered if the car in the driveway was the teenager's.

Before getting out of the unmarked, Pete called her cell.

When Sydney answered, he explained that he and his partner had some additional questions. He asked if she was home.

Sydney's yes sounded more like a question than an answer.

"We'll be there shortly," Pete said.

Seconds later, a teenage girl made a beeline to the car parked at the end of the driveway. She appeared to be about sixteen. She was twenty pounds overweight with a pretty face.

Pete and Martin got out of the unmarked and ran to the car in the driveway.

Sydney saw them, rushed and beat them to the car. She was getting in when Pete reached the driver's-side door.

He stood inside the open door, keeping Sydney from closing it.

"Let me introduce myself," he said. He displayed his badge and ID, and gave his name. He introduced Martin, who by then stood alongside him.

"It looks like you decided you prefer to talk out here," Pete said.

"No, it isn't that. I can't find the notebook I use to log my assignments. Thought I might've left it in here."

"I'm surprised you decided to put on a jacket and scarf, and grab your gloves and purse to do that," Pete said.

Sydney's face reddened, possibly due to the outdoor temperature. The embarrassed look on her face indicated otherwise.

"How old are you?" Pete asked.

"Eighteen."

"Do you want to talk out here, or in the house?" Pete asked.

"Here's fine."

"Okay, but it might take an hour," Pete said.

Sydney raised an eyebrow and displayed a "you've got to be kidding me" look. She blew out a breath that created a cloud of steam and slowly extracted herself from the car.

At the front door, she reached for the knob, then paused. Before opening the door, she turned to look at Pete and Martin. She seemed to be contemplating.

Pete wondered if she was calculating the likely success of an attempt to get inside and slam the door in their faces.

FORTY-SIX

Turning back to the door, Sydney opened it and held it while Pete and Martin entered.

She took off her shoes in the entryway and walked into the living room.

It was compact. The wooden floors looked real, and the area rug in the center of the room matched the greens and yellows of the furniture.

Without a word, Sydney removed her jacket, dropped it on a chair, and plopped down on the loveseat. Then she stared at the two investigators.

"May we come in?" Pete asked.

"I guess."

Pete and Martin walked into the living room, and sat down in the two chairs that faced Sydney.

"I already talked to you today. Why are you here?" Sydney asked.

"Is that your car in the driveway, Sydney?" Martin asked.

"Yes. I know it's not much, but it is mine."

Pete already knew the make and model. It was a rust-eaten, red Honda Accord.

"What was that all about?" Martin asked.

"What do you mean?" Sydney assumed a puzzled expression.

"Attempting to leave when you knew we were on our way," Martin said.

"I told you, I went out to the car to look for my notebook."

"And I know that isn't true, so tell me the reason you tried to avoid us. Otherwise, we'll take you to headquarters and discuss it there," Martin threatened.

"Okay, fine. Everyone knows something's happening with Dylan. I don't know what. I do know it's bad. I don't want to take a chance at hurting him, and I don't know what will hurt him. I didn't want to talk to you before I found out."

"You and Dylan go to different high schools," Pete said. "How did you meet?"

"Dylan's friend Logan knows a lot of kids at Warren. I met him through them."

"Specifically?" Pete asked.

"I'm not sure. It's been years. Probably Noah Wilkin. We used to hang." Sydney looked regretful.

"What's your typical weekday schedule?" Martin asked.

"Mom and Dad won't let me drive to school. I have to catch the bus at six thirty. School doesn't even start 'til seven thirty. I have to get up at about five thirty. How crazy is that?"

"What if you miss the bus?" Martin asked.

"Mom or Dad has to drive me. Then I'm late for school, and I hear about it the whole way there."

Sydney said she wasn't late for school any days this week, and today was the only day she missed school.

Martin and Pete knew that. They'd already checked with the offices at Warren and Anderson. All of the students on their list, including Dylan Norman, were in their first period class on Tuesday.

"Between yesterday and today, how many times have you either spoken with or texted Dylan?" Pete asked.

"Twice."

"Did you talk, or text?" Pete asked.

"Texted last night. Talked this morning."

The information forensics was obtaining would either support or contradict that claim, but Pete didn't yet have those results. If necessary, he could call and get them before they left.

"What did you talk and text about?" Martin asked.

"School, stuff like that."

"Do you know the price you could pay for lying to us?" Martin asked.

"No."

"Jail. Want to go check it out?" Martin asked.

Sydney sprang to an upright position for the first time since they arrived. She was wide-eyed and looked scared. "No, I don't want to go to jail. Dylan wanted a ride—both times."

"Where did he want you to take him?" Martin asked.

"I don't know. I'm not sure he knew. He was upset. He didn't say."

"Why was he upset?" Martin asked.

"About the police going to his house and questioning everyone."

"Why did that upset him?" Martin asked.

"Well, *duh*. You're questioning me, and I'm upset. No one wants to talk to the police."

"No one? Or just people who have something to hide?" Martin asked.

"I don't have anything to hide. It's just that no one wants to be hounded by you."

"You didn't ask why he wanted to run?" Martin asked.

"No."

"If I asked for that kind of favor, I'd feel compelled to tell my friend why I needed the favor. There aren't many kids who'd skip out on school with no idea what they were getting into, are there?" Martin asked.

"I asked. He said there wasn't time to talk."

"There wasn't time to talk because he had to call Logan, didn't he?" Martin asked.

"Yes. How did you know?"

Martin didn't know before he asked that question.

"How well do you know Logan Clay?" Martin asked.

"Not very. I do know he and Dylan are practically Siamese twins."

"I hear Logan plans to go to Notre Dame," Martin said.

"In his dreams."

"Why do you say that?" Martin asked.

"I heard he wasn't accepted, but I don't want to be arrested for being wrong."

Pete and Martin expected to see a smart-ass smile. Sydney fooled them.

"Does Logan have a car?" Martin asked.

"Yes, but he doesn't drive to school, either."

"When was the last time you saw or spoke with Logan?" Martin asked.

"Last weekend. A bunch of us got together."

"Do you know Ellie Cook?" Martin asked.

"Yes. She's Dylan's girlfriend."

"Do you know Kevin Douglas?" Pete asked.

"I've heard the name, but I can't place it. Does he go to Anderson?"

"I'm not sure," Pete said. "He might work at the Cambridge Garden Center."

Sydney smiled. "Oh, then Logan probably mentioned him. He works at Cambridge some nights and weekends."

"How long has Logan worked there?" Pete asked.

"Since last fall, I think. I'm not positive."

FORTY-SEVEN

Pete dialed Logan Clay's cell while Martin called his home. It was six thirty in the evening. The home phone was answered by Logan's sister. She didn't know where Logan was, but thought he should be home soon.

Martin asked if anyone else was home, and Logan's mother picked up the phone. He explained that he and his partner had some questions for Logan, and wanted to know where they could find him.

She said he should have been home, but was often late. She seemed unconcerned and invited them to wait for Logan at their home.

Pete's call to Logan's cell was greeted by voicemail.

Martin drove to the street where Logan and his family lived. He again parked several houses away, to avoid giving Logan a reason to flee, should that be his reaction to another meeting with them.

The Clay family lived about a mile east of Lake Phalen, and within four miles of both Anderson High School and the crime scene. Their house was one of a handful of new homes, encroaching on a neighborhood where the houses were decades older and significantly smaller. "Don't know why we always have to park down the street from the people we're visiting," Martin kidded. "I'm amazed we're not always welcomed with open arms."

"I don't know about you, Martin. More often than not, my family runs the other way when they see me coming."

"That's only because your dad fears the day you show up to take away his car."

"Ouch, Martin, did my dad call you?"

"No. Are you actually considering it? Your dad seems mentally and physically fit."

"He is, but it's a looming threat—for both of us. I hope it never happens."

Logan's mother answered the door. She had carrot-red hair. Her upturned nose and freckles made her look a bit like a large leprechaun. A bright green sweater furthered the impression of an Irish influence.

"I understand you've been talking to some of the kids at Anderson," she said. "My daughter said you already spoke with Logan today." She looked nervous. "Did Logan do something?"

"We've spent the day interviewing people," Martin said. "Now we're speaking with some of them a second time. We want to interview Logan again. It's important. I'm confident we can count on your cooperation. If you have a way to speed up your son's arrival, please do."

"My husband might know where he is. Give me a minute. I'll call him."

As she picked up a phone, Martin asked, "Where is your husband?"

She delayed dialing and said, "He's at work. I don't expect him for about an hour."

"Where does he work?" Martin asked.

"He's the manager at Kitker's Hardware in Roseville."

"Okay. Please call and see if he's heard from Logan," Martin said.

After explaining that the police were at their home and looking for Logan, Ms. Clay asked if he spoke with their son after school.

He didn't. He said he would leave immediately and be home as soon as possible.

When she conveyed that information, Pete told her to tell him to stay where he was. He and his partner would meet with him there.

The hardware store was a large-scale operation in a strip mall. As Martin drove up, he and Pete saw a man standing inside the doorway.

He was a few inches taller than average. An inactive life or a love for food was taking a toll on his waistline. His dark hair was thinning, and his readers were halfway down his nose.

As they got out of the unmarked car, the man exited the store asking, "Police, right?"

"Yes, sir," Pete said. "We want to speak with your son. Any idea where he might be?"

"I don't know. I think Dylan Norman might know. I tried to reach Logan. He didn't answer his cell."

"Let's go inside," Pete said. "Do you have an office?"

"Yes, but the store is virtually empty. Can't we just step inside the door and talk?"

Once they did as requested, Pete continued, "Do you and Logan fish or hunt together?"

"Yes. We always fish in the Brainerd Lakes area. We often hunt up there as well."

"Where do you stay when you're there?" Pete asked.

"My friends and I own a cabin. We call it our hunting shack. It's pretty minimal."

"But it provides heat and protection from the elements?" Pete asked.

"Yes, we've spent many winter weekends there. What's this about? Do you suspect my son of something? If you do, don't you have to tell me?"

"I'll suspect him of something if he disappears," Pete said.

"I sent him a text right after my wife called. When he's with friends, he tends to be better about responding to texts than answering the phone. I haven't heard from him, but that's not particularly unusual. I'm sure he's with friends and lost track of the time. I'll try calling him. We're very close. I'm sure I'd know if he was in trouble." Contrary to the nonchalance he attempted to convey, Clay looked worried.

He pulled a cell out of a pants pocket. First he called home to ensure Logan hadn't arrived. He thought his wife would have called, but... He disconnected, sighed, and dialed his son's cell.

Pete figured the delay meant the call went to voicemail when Logan's father began speaking, "Logan, where are you?"

He listened intently for a minute, nodding occasionally, then said, "Son, I'll be there in fifteen minutes. Don't go anywhere, okay?"

Logan's father closed his phone and said, "He's at Dylan's house. He said Dylan was arrested. Was he?"

"Yes, sir," Pete said. He didn't explain.

Logan's father looked inquisitive and worried, but he didn't ask for an explanation. He drove to the Norman home.

Pete rode with him to prevent any unmonitored conversations between father and son, including one telling Logan to flee.

The entire trip, Clay's hands moved nervously back and forth over the steering wheel, and his fingers tap danced to a melody Pete couldn't hear. Despite the urgency of the situation, Clay's speed was locked onto the posted limits.

Pete believed his presence in the car, and having Martin following in the unmarked, prevented Logan's dad from following his instincts.

There was no conversation in the car, giving Pete plenty of time to think on the way to the Norman home. Would Logan wait there for his dad? How would Logan and his dad react to his and Martin's questions? Would Logan's dad call an attorney? Probably.

At the moment, they had nothing to prove Logan was involved. It looked like he lied about his plans to go to Notre Dame. If so, why? Was Sydney Brown wrong about that? The only thing tying Logan to the case was his friendship with Dylan.

Could he and Martin get Logan to open up? If they did, how much would that help? How many people other than Dylan were involved?

If Dylan refused to talk, was there evidence in the LeSabre that would lead them to all participants? Should Kevin Douglas be their next contact? There appeared to be a connection between Kevin and Logan. Was it coincidental?

FORTY-EIGHT

Martin parked behind Clay's car, on the street in front of Dylan's home. It looked like every light in the house was on.

Before the two investigators permitted Logan's father to ring the doorbell, Martin surveyed the house and yard, getting the lay of the land. Then, after conferring with Pete, he positioned himself so he and Pete covered all reasonable exits.

Pete stood behind Logan's dad, at the bottom of the steps to the front door.

Clay observed all this. His sour expression and fidgeting conveyed impatience.

When Pete nodded, Clay rang the doorbell.

Seconds later, Logan opened the door. With outstretched arms, he invited a hug from his dad. The gesture was cut short when Logan spotted Pete.

In one quick motion, Logan grabbed his dad's shoulders and spun, trading places. Then he leaped over the railing and onto the grass. His weight and the marginally frozen ground slowed him—but barely.

Pete yelled, "Martin!" and took off after Logan.

With the shot of adrenalin that accompanies fear, Logan was off at top speed.

Pete's speed was attributable to training and sheer desire.

Logan wore running shoes and sweats. He was dressed for this sort of thing.

Pete wore dress shoes and a suit. He wasn't.

They ran down the sidewalk, heading east from the Norman home. Thanks to the spacing of streetlights, despite the absence of leaves, sizeable trees cast shadows that threw segments of the path into utter darkness. Although Pete lifted his feet high enough to avoid tripping, an occasional dip or bump jarred his otherwise smooth gait.

If the decision was Pete's, he wouldn't have selected this route. Since it was out of his hands, he did what he could to maximize the likelihood of success.

Contemplating Martin's comment about *NUMB3RS*, he wondered what Charlie Eppes would recommend at a time like this.

Was Logan leading him into a trap? That would explain why Logan took off, running—a seemingly illogical act. Had he arranged something with friends, just in case, because he anticipated his dad bringing the cops? If so, wouldn't he leave before his dad arrived? Logan appeared shocked when he saw Pete standing behind his dad. The halted hug fit with that. Was it scripted? He knew nothing about Logan's half of the conversation, when his dad called from the hardware store. Was Logan's dad silent all the way to Dylan's home, because he was mulling over something Logan said?

What about Paul Norman? He didn't bother to mask his animosity toward Pete. Was he capable of reacting, unthinkingly, and becoming an accomplice? That would be reactionary, and it would do nothing to help Dylan. Just the same...

Pete's ears were attuned to any unexpected or unusual sounds. The wind didn't help, nor did the people who didn't rake their leaves. With assistance from the wind, the dried leaves skittered across and along the sidewalks, creating a scratching sound that could mask more ominous sounds. Pete listened intently for any inconsistencies.

With eyes and ears attuned to the possibility of sabotage, Pete carefully evaluated their path, looking for all potential staging points.

He sped up, determined to bring this game to an end before Logan, his father, Paul Norman, or anyone else did anything crazy.

The temperature wasn't as warm as Tuesday. Pete saw puffs of steam as he exhaled into the cold air. Thankfully, this temperature wasn't extreme enough in either direction to affect his speed or endurance.

The distance between boy and man closed—gradually, while Pete worked out the details of his plan. After chasing Logan for another hundred yards, he was close enough.

With a burst of speed, he pulled alongside the boy. After taking a deep breath, he executed a flying tackle.

Logan's football training kicked in. He made an evasive move.

Pete connected with the sidewalk. He rolled and was quickly back on his feet, running.

That failed effort put about fifteen yards between Logan and him.

Pete maintained this distance and reevaluated his options.

Martin was a part of this, yet Pete hadn't seen him since the chase began. It would help to know what Martin was thinking and doing. Where was he?

Endurance was Pete's strong suit. He knew speed was Dylan's. What was Logan's? Did high school football and baseball players train for endurance? It might depend on the position a kid played. What positions did Logan play?

No doubt the kid was scared. Fear contorted Logan's face as he went over the railing and took off. Was he depending on his dad to save him? If so, the kid probably read the way it unfolded as a betrayal. Did he think his dad was throwing him to the wolves? Was this chase no more than the old fight-or-flight reflex?

Pete thought about his reaction if, as a teenager, he found himself in Logan's position. He figured it would start with despair and go south. Would he run from the police? Possibly. Would he lead them into a trap? Never. He was certain of that.

If he ran, he'd run as fast and as far as he could. He wouldn't stop until he collapsed—or until his brain kicked in, overriding the adrenaline rush. If and when his brain took charge, what would he do?

What if Logan was nothing like him? What if despair or anger caused the boy to do something stupid? Pete regretted not using the trip from the hardware store to Dylan's house to find out more about Logan.

He also wished he knew if the size of the kid's forearms was attributable to steroids. A person on steroids could be more explosive.

Was Logan a party to the attack on Rice? If not, how much did he know? Ellie Cook and Sydney Brown each said Logan and Dylan were inseparable. How far would Logan go to protect Dylan and vice versa?

Logan's dad drove past, and began keeping pace with his son.

"Son, stop, please!" his father yelled.

Logan ignored him.

His dad continued pleading.

Logan responded by leaving the sidewalk. He cut between two houses, and began running through backyards.

Following the boy's path, Pete hoped Logan would soon return to sidewalks. Granted he and Martin made several trips to this neighborhood over the past four days. Even so, he didn't know the landscape well enough to run full throttle after dark. Unfortunately, memorizing the landscape wasn't a priority at the time.

Due to his friendship with Dylan, it was likely that Logan was familiar with the yards in this neighborhood. Unfortunately for Pete, the benefits that afforded soon became apparent.

Logan ran to and cleared a chest-high fence without missing a beat.

Pete saw the fence well in advance, having witnessed Logan's leap. Instead of going over the fence, should he run around it? The yard was sizable and filled with stuff. In addition to a massive storage shed, there were numerous pine trees and bushes. Would those items camouflage the kid, if he took the easy route? Was Logan counting on that?

Leather soled shoes added nothing to his effort to scale the fence. He made it, and was grateful this chase wasn't videotaped. Conquering that fence was just the beginning.

His presence in the fenced backyard was greeted by a deep-throated growl. Did the massive dog recognize Logan, who was now clearing the fence on the far side of the yard? It didn't make a sound when the kid encroached on its space. Now, however, the dog had its sights set on Pete.

Pete knew it was important not to display fear. He could talk calmly to the dog, holding out a hand. Like hell! The growl and the teeth someone's "best friend" displayed were an adequate deterrent.

He was back over the fence in record time, at least for him. In the process, he left a sample of his pant leg and a bit of DNA on the fence. After picking himself up off the ground for the second time in minutes, he continued the pursuit, staying outside the fence. As he went, he searched desperately for the kid.

Pete was confident Logan knew about his encounter with the dog. Had the kid hoped the dog would end his pursuit? If so, since that didn't happen, what was next in the boy's bag of tricks?

Inadvisable as it felt, and despite the blisters forming on his feet, Pete ran full throttle, desperate to catch a glimpse of the kid, before it was too late. Even so, his mind raced significantly faster than his feet.

Was the kid now far enough ahead to be out of sight and hearing range?

If Logan was smart enough to get into Notre Dame, he had a head on his shoulders. That being the case, there was thought going into the path the kid selected.

Was he heading for a hiding place? That was an option only if Pete was unable to see the boy duck into it. Hence, now was the perfect time for Logan to head for cover. Had he done that?

Was Pete running into a trap? That being the case, the distance now between him and Logan might give him a fighting chance of detecting the trap before it sprung on him.

On the other hand, did Pete's double encounter with the fence give the kid the perfect opportunity to change his route, returning to the sidewalks? Seemed risky with Martin and Mr. Clay cruising the streets, looking for both of them.

Crossing the street two blocks beyond his encounter with the dog, Pete saw Martin in the unmarked.

Martin rolled down the window, as Pete approached.

"What happened to you?" Martin asked, referring to Pete's appearance.

Running toward him, Pete panted, "Not now. Go east. Four blocks. Kid can't be beyond that. Park. Head this way, through yards. Hope one of us sees him, before we see each other."

Feeling more optimistic, Pete resumed the chase. As he crossed the street at dog plus block five, a backyard spotlight snapped on.

With a wave of optimism, Pete wondered if Logan tripped a motion detector. Optimistically, the odds were fifty-fifty.

Pete was near exhaustion, but resolute. Drawing on every ounce of energy he could muster, he kicked it up a notch, scrambling toward the light. He had to get there before the kid was beyond the illuminated yard.

A half-block away from his target, Pete saw the boy.

Logan stood in the well-lit backyard, looking all around. Was he trying to determine whether the light revealed his location to Pete? If so, it could prove to be his biggest mistake of the night. A moment later, the boy's eyes locked on his pursuer.

Logan shot left, toward the street.

Pete cut left along a parallel path, reaching the sidewalk little more than a second after the boy.

With Pete on his left, Logan had no choice—unless he wanted to give up. He went right, running down the sidewalk.

Where was Martin?

Logan took another left.

Pete wondered if hopes of help from another dog dictated this move. Or was Logan intent on using a better running surface to extend the distance between them, before returning to backyards?

Nearing the corner where Logan went left, Pete saw another reason.

Martin trotted down the sidewalk, in pursuit of the boy.

As Pete turned the corner, still roughly a half-block behind the boy, he saw what could prove to be either a blessing or a curse.

Logan's dad came around the corner—driving toward his son and the two investigators.

Over his shoulder, Pete yelled, "Martin, get the car!" He prepared to follow Logan's next detour.

Logan surprised him. He didn't alter his path.

What did that mean? What was the kid doing? Was he going to get into his dad's car? If he did, would he attempt to take control of it? If not, would his dad assist Logan? Or Martin and him—assuming they were mutually exclusive?

Logan did a quick swerve. He ran around his dad's car and toward the driver's side.

What happened next shocked Pete.

Logan's dad waited until Logan reached the back bumper. Then he simultaneously threw the driver's side door open and slammed on the brakes.

Unable to stop on a dime, Logan piled into the door.

Pete heard the impact, as Logan's momentum and weight tested the door's hinges.

Clay's action shocked Logan and broke his spirit. Pain and exhaustion likely contributed. Logan bent at the waist, gasping and trying to talk.

"Dad, Dad," he moaned. Panting, he added, "How could you?"

FORTY-NINE

Before Logan's dad was out of his car, Pete had his son handcuffed. Logan didn't resist.

"Logan, I did it to help you," his dad pleaded. "I had to do it before this went too far. Why did you run?"

Logan was still bent forward. Still gasping for air. He either didn't attempt or didn't bother to speak.

"We're taking him to headquarters," Pete panted.

"Logan, I'll get you an attorney. Don't say anything until he's there. Okay, son?"

Logan looked at the ground, not at his dad. He didn't answer.

"*Please*, Logan. Do what I ask." He tried to look his son in the eye.

Logan didn't cooperate. He added to his father's pain by refusing to acknowledge him.

Logan's dad turned his attention to Pete. "Officer, is this about the accident on Wheelock?"

Pete nodded. He, too, was winded.

"I know Logan was home. Why are you arresting him?"

"Because of his actions. We're taking Logan to headquarters. We're going to interview him." Pete's answer was divided into several short bursts, interrupted by quick breaths.

"Which actions are you talking about?"

Martin pulled alongside Pete and got out of the unmarked.

With a protective hand on the top of the boy's head, Pete loaded Logan into the backseat.

Logan's dad continued pleading with his son and the investigators. His arms flew as he attempted to get someone's, anyone's, attention. The more he talked, the louder his voice became. "Can't you talk to him at our home? Why are you doing this? Don't you have to answer my questions before hauling my son away?"

Failing to get anywhere with Pete or Martin, Clay redirected his pleas. After getting as close as possible to the back window of the unmarked, he began yelling.

"Please, Logan, don't throw your life away. I'm getting an attorney. Don't say a word before I get there. You don't have to say anything before you have an attorney. Do you hear me? *Please*, Logan, tell me you'll do as I ask!"

Logan sat in the unmarked, with his back to his dad. He didn't nod or shake his head.

The two investigators gave Clay the opportunity to say that much. Then they got in the unmarked and drove away.

FIFTY

The two investigators left Logan's dad standing in the middle of the street, looking devastated.

When they reached headquarters, Pete and Martin followed the same drill they used with Dylan. They took Logan to Homicide and put him in an interview room.

For the record, Pete stated the date and location, and asked Logan his name and age. Once again, video and audio equipment recorded everything.

"I'm Logan Clay. I'm eighteen."

Pete Mirandized Logan and explained they might be able to work a deal if Logan cooperated.

"I don't need a deal!" Logan shouted. "I didn't do anything! My dad said to wait for his attorney. Screw that! Ask your stupid questions. I just want to get this over and go home."

Logan's body language said as much as his words. By the time he finished that speech, his face was beet red.

"Your dad claimed he knew you were home Tuesday morning. He said he knows you're innocent. Based on... ?" Pete asked.

"Based on the facts. It's the truth!"

"You told us you wouldn't get involved because you've spent your life working to get into Notre Dame. I hear you left out one small detail. You already received your denial of admission," Pete said.

"No, I didn't! Who told you that? It's a lie! I didn't follow the early action process. A couple of my friends did and got denials. I won't get a decision until early April." Sweat rolled off Logan's face.

"You just wrote your own denial," Pete said. "Did you plan to play football at Notre Dame? Think about it, being a member of the Fighting Irish. I guess that'll eat away at you every single day, while you serve out your life sentence. I feel sorry for you, pal. An ill-planned, vicious attack on an innocent stranger effectively flushed your life down the toilet. Dylan told us how you turned his plan for an innocent act into a malicious attack," Pete continued.

"No, he didn't! Dylan isn't a liar, and he'd never try to pin it on me!" Logan was up and out of the chair, spitting fire.

"How else would we know it was you?" Pete asked. "Dylan plea-bargained to reduce his sentence. That's the only reason he told us. He did his best to protect you, but life in prison is a high price to pay for friendship."

"Let me talk to him. I have to talk to Dylan!" Logan said, slamming his fists on the table.

"So the two of you can work out the details of your story? No way. That's not how it works," Pete said. "After you talk to us, perhaps we'll let you talk to him. Definitely not before."

"I don't believe anything you're saying. I don't believe Dylan would do this to me." Logan's face was flushed and drenched with sweat.

"Dylan was looking at either life or five years in prison. He did the right thing, even though you're his best friend," Pete said.

"If he's pointing the finger at me, I know why. But I still don't believe you."

Pete wondered at what point Logan would change his mind, deciding he wanted an attorney. "Dylan feels bad for Nicholas Rice's children. He decided it's important that justice is served—for their sake," he explained.

"If that's what he's doing, why wouldn't he tell the truth? Why would he say it was me and not Caitlin?" Logan looked exasperated. "Why would she be willing to let this happen to Dylan and me? That's what I want to know."

"What's that supposed to mean?" Pete asked.

"Caitlin was the one who was furious with Mrs. Rice. Dylan doesn't have his dad on a pedestal. He was angry with his dad. Not with Mrs. Rice, much less her husband. How would hurting Mr. Rice make things better? The only people who could fix things were Dylan's parents."

Logan sank in the chair. He seemed exhausted after that speech.

"What makes you think Caitlin could do it?" Pete asked. "We spoke with her. She's smart. She's an excellent athlete..."

"Yeah," Logan interrupted. "She's always on the honor roll because everything comes easy to her. And she's such a good athlete because she's on steroids!"

"That's a rotten thing to say without proof. Do you have proof or are you just passing the buck?" Martin asked.

"It's true. She's gotten more and more angry. Ask Dylan. I'm sure you know that's what people on steroids do! Second thought, don't bother asking Dylan. If he's going to prison for her, he'll lie about that, too."

"Dylan told you his sister's on steroids?" Martin asked.

Logan didn't answer. He rested his head on his right hand, and ran his other hand back and forth through his hair.

"How long ago did he tell you that?" Martin asked.

Logan stared silently at the floor.

"If all this is true, you had no reason to run. Why did you run when we only wanted to talk to you?" Martin asked.

"I already talked to you today. Why did you have to talk to me again?"

"If you weren't involved in the attack on Rice, why were you afraid to answer a few more questions?" Pete asked.

"I called Dylan about a hundred times today. He never answered. I wanted to talk to him first. That's why I went to his house."

"Yet you knew Dylan was in jail. You planned to hide for the rest of your life?" Martin asked.

"No. I went to Dylan's to find out why he wouldn't answer his cell. His dad told me he was in jail. He said you couldn't keep him there more than thirty-six hours. I just had to hide until he got out. When Dad called, I thought he'd help me. I never thought he'd turn me in. If I'd known what he planned, I'd have left before he got there!" Logan's face was scarlet, and he was soaking wet. He looked like he'd just climbed out of a swimming pool.

"Why did you have to talk to Dylan before you talked to us again?" Pete asked.

"You came to school and asked all kinds of questions. I know you talked to Ellie, Noah, and Justin. Dylan didn't show up at school today. I wanted to know what was happening."

"And you wanted to know that so you could get your stories straight?" Pete asked.

"No, I just wanted to know that he was okay. I wanted to know if you did something to him. Turns out you did. Dylan didn't do anything. I'd know if he did. He'd have talked to me about it. He'd have asked for my help."

"How did Caitlin react to her brother's arrest?" Pete asked.

"I don't know. I haven't seen her all day."

"She wasn't home when you got there?" Pete asked.

"I don't know. All I know is that I saw her mom and dad, but I didn't see her."

Logan was released, pending investigation.

FIFTY-ONE

Pete glanced at his watch as he and Martin pulled up in front of the Norman home. It was nine o'clock. He rang the doorbell, while Martin watched the house from the street corner fifty feet away.

Paul Norman came to the door. He was furious. "You've already got my son in jail. What more could you possibly want?"

"My partner and I are going to question your daughter at headquarters. Caitlin will ride with us. Either you or your wife will be permitted in the interview room, while we question her."

"I'm going to call my attorney."

"That, sir, is up to you."

"We'll be there as soon as possible," Paul snarled. "Remember, dammit, you can't start questioning Caitlin before we get there."

"Get your daughter," Pete said.

Paul Norman returned, looking like he wanted to take Pete's head off. Caitlin stood far behind him, looking as limp as a rag doll.

"Get your jacket, Caitlin," Pete said.

When Caitlin reappeared, Pete and Martin took her to the unmarked and loaded her in the backseat. Pete drove, and Martin rode in back with Caitlin.

Caitlin's father was allowed in the interview room with his daughter and her attorney. Ordinarily it would have been either Paul or the attorney. Both were permitted only because Paul swore that otherwise he'd file charges of coercion. He insisted he knew Caitlin, like Dylan, was innocent.

As soon as Caitlin, her father, her attorney, and the two investigators were all in the interview room, Pete started with the Miranda warning. Then he asked the girl's name and age.

"My name is Caitlin Norman. I'm sixteen."

"Your brother put his neck on the chopping block for you, Caitlin," Pete began.

"Stop right there," her attorney demanded, slamming a fist on the table. "Did you bring her here to lecture her about some trumped-up charges or are you going to question her?"

"It takes a very special brother to do something like that," Pete continued, unaffected by the attorney's protests. "Dylan confessed. He could get life..."

"Don't listen to him, Caitlin," her attorney instructed. "He's lying to you. He can't prove anything. That's why he's doing this. They won't be able to keep Dylan in jail."

"Dylan's eighteen," Pete continued. "That means he'll be tried as an adult."

Caitlin stared at Pete. Tears streamed down her cheeks.

"Tell me what happened, Caitlin," Pete said.

"Don't tell him anything but your name and address!" the attorney insisted.

"I understand you've been very upset about your father's affair," Pete said. "I heard..."

Caitlin's dad and her attorney looked furious.

"We're leaving," the attorney said, pushing his glasses up on a nose that bore signs of years of excessive drinking. "Caitlin, Paul, let's go." He stood and put his hands on the back of Caitlin's chair, trying to pull it away from the table.

Paul Norman looked relieved.

"I'm not going with you," Caitlin declared.

Paul's smile faded.

"That doesn't make any sense, Caitlin. I'm an attorney. I know what he's doing. I can protect you if you allow me to do my job. Look what happened to Dylan. It wouldn't have happened if I'd been there. Don't make the same mistake your brother made."

"You were here this afternoon, remember?" Pete asked the attorney. "Dylan didn't want your help, either."

"Caitlin, he doesn't have any evidence," the attorney sneered. "Hence, there won't be a trial."

"I don't want him to be my attorney," Caitlin said, pointing. "I don't want my dad here, either. I just want to talk to you and your partner. Can I do that?" Caitlin sniffled.

"Yes. We'd like to help you, Caitlin," Pete said. "Will you let us help you?"

"You'll be making a terrible mistake," her attorney insisted.

"Caitlin, please, let me stay," Paul pleaded.

"Only if you let me talk and promise not to interrupt, Dad. If you won't promise, I don't want you here. And Dad, I don't think you're going to want to hear what I have to say." Caitlin put her hand over her mouth and looked at her dad for the first time since he arrived in the interview room.

Paul Norman sat down.

The attorney slammed his chair against the table, and exited the interview room.

Martin escorted him out of the homicide area. On Martin's way back to the interview room, an investigator stopped him.

"Didn't think the commander would stop to check the text sent a few minutes ago." Handing a note to Martin, he added. "He's going to want to see this."

FIFTY-TWO

Martin handed the note to Pete.

Pete glanced at it and nodded. Then he turned to Caitlin and began, "First, Caitlin, before you say anything, I want to remind you that you have the right to have an attorney present during this and any future questioning. I want to make sure that's clear to you."

"Yes, sir, I understand. I don't want an attorney. I just want to tell you what happened. Then, if you're willing, I'd like you to help me. But I doubt you'll be willing, once I tell you."

"Start at the beginning, Caitlin," Pete said. "What was your involvement in this?"

"I drove the car. I hit Mr. Rice. I didn't plan to kill him. I didn't want to kill him," Caitlin moaned.

"How did it happen, Caitlin?" Pete asked.

Caitlin rested her chin on her left hand and began in a shaky voice, "Mom found out that Dad had this thing with Mrs. Rice. She was furious. They started fighting all the time. I hated being around them. Mom even began hassling Dylan and me for everything we did and didn't do. Nothing was right or good enough. She was angry all the time and with everyone."

Paul Norman grimaced.

"Dylan and I tried to get away from it. We stayed with friends more often, but Mom only allowed us to do that on weekends. Then she decided we couldn't be gone all weekend every weekend. Dylan said Mom might be willing to let us stay with her mother. When he asked Grandma, she said it would be a problem with school and sports and everything. She was right, of course. She suggested we spend more time with friends and try to ignore Mom and Dad. Yeah, right." Caitlin's head bobbed. She looked dejected.

"It got so I couldn't deal with the fighting. I started crying all the time. I couldn't concentrate on anything but the problems at home. I haven't gotten my grades yet, but I think I blew finals. I had to find a way to fix it. I had to get things back to normal. No one else was doing it. I started by thinking of ways to make Mom happy. I knew leaving my junk around the house bugged her. I made sure I always put my stuff away. I put Dylan's stuff away, too. I helped Mom with dinner and the dishes whenever I was home. I did everything I could think of. It didn't help. I don't think Mom even noticed. Things kept getting worse."

Tears streamed down Caitlin's cheeks.

After taking a deep breath, she continued. "I was desperate to find a solution. Each time I did, I realized it was either unreasonable or undoable. Then I had an idea. You know how people sometimes treat their kids better if something happens to a friend's kid?" Caitlin looked at Pete, then Martin.

Martin nodded, and Pete's chin dipped an inch or two.

"One of my cousins was diagnosed with cancer," she continued. "For a month or more, Mom couldn't have been nicer to Dylan and me. Well, I wasn't wishing cancer on anyone. I knew it wasn't the same, but shouldn't that kind of reaction apply to your husband, too? I thought Mom would forgive Dad if something happened to Mr. Rice. I thought she'd start thinking past what Dad did. I also hoped knowing Mrs. Rice was hurting would help."

"What made you think Heather Rice still cared about her husband?" Pete asked.

"I overheard Dad telling Mom that Mr. Rice forgave his wife. Dad said they still love each other."

"Based on the example you gave us, I'm surprised you didn't do something to one of the Rice children, rather than Nicholas Rice," Pete said.

"Dylan and I were hurting. I figured the Rice kids were, too. Besides, they're little kids. I'm not that kind of monster." That statement appeared to trigger a realization. Caitlin's hand shot up and covered her mouth.

"Why target Nicholas Rice? Why not his wife?" Pete asked.

"For lots of reasons." Caitlin began counting them off on her fingers. "First, like I said, I hoped knowing someone else's husband, especially Mrs. Rice's husband, was hurt would make Mom appreciate Dad again. I hoped for that reason she'd love him again and forgive him. Second, I knew Mr. Rice was a runner. I sometimes saw him running months before any of this happened. I never saw his wife, so he was easier to reach. Third, the fact he ran early in the morning, when few people are out. Fourth, lots of times, such as when someone you love gets cancer, people say, 'I wish it was me. I wish I could trade places.' By hurting Mr. Rice, not his wife, I figured his wife would suffer more. Finally, I thought Mom might back off if Mrs. Rice was punished. You hear it all the time on TV. People believe having the criminal punished will make them feel better. I knew what happened was Mrs. Rice's fault. She hit on my dad. I'm sure Mom knows that, too." Caitlin looked at her dad, perhaps hoping for affirmation.

Paul's head dropped. The only signal he provided was a failure to meet her gaze.

Caitlin wiped her eyes and returned her attention to Pete and Martin. "Dylan tried to help, but nothing he said or did made a difference. I couldn't sleep. I fixated on that stupid solution. I lay in bed at night, planning every detail a thousand different ways." Caitlin dissolved in body-racking sobs.

Paul Norman looked like he was fighting back tears.

"I understand you've been taking steroids," Pete said.

Caitlin's eyes went wide. "That's crazy! Do you know what they do to your mind and your body? I wanted to go into medical research. I'd never have risked taking them and destroying my chances of making a difference!" She paused as reality sank in. "I found an even worse way to do that." She covered her face with her hands and broke down.

Paul Norman continued to comply with his daughter's requirement that he remain silent. Even so, his facial expressions conveyed disbelief and horror.

After several seconds, Pete continued. "Tell me how you planned to hurt Nicholas Rice."

"I tried and tried to think of a way to hurt him just enough to hurt his wife. I don't know what made me think of bumping him with a car. All I know is, the more I thought about it, the more I thought I could do it. I spent a lot of time planning all the details. I had to succeed. Instead," sniff, "I totally blew it."

"How did you know that Nicholas Rice would be at that place at that time?" Pete asked.

"When I saw Mr. Rice running, it was always before school. Mom and Dad knew I often ran before school. That made it easy to leave early in the morning. I ran to Mr. Rice's home early several mornings, hoping to see him before I had to go home and get ready for school. One morning, I saw him running toward his house. I knew I had to be there earlier the next time. After that, I spent a lot of time figuring out where he ran and when. I was always running or pretending to run when he saw me. I'd wave and say 'hi,' so he wouldn't get suspicious."

"How did you recognize Nicholas Rice? How did you know you were following him and not someone else?" Pete asked.

"I met him once and remembered him. To make sure I had the right person, I watched him run to and go into his house that first morning I saw him. I knew it was the Rice house. I looked it up on the Internet."

"Tell me the last two times, the times before last Tuesday, when you watched him," Pete said.

Paul stared at the floor.

"Last Monday, and last week on Wednesday."

"Both of those times you met or saw him while he was running?" Pete asked.

"No," Caitlin looked embarrassed. "Last week, Wednesday, I was in his backyard, finding out for sure when he got up and left to go running. I didn't always see him at the same time. I didn't know if that was because he didn't always run the same places, or because he didn't always start at the same time. I was sure if I knew that, I'd be able to find him when the time came."

"You were confident you could determine that by watching his house just once?" Pete asked.

"No, you only asked about the last two times. I went to his back-yard and watched to see what time he got up and left the two weeks before last, too. I did it a different day each week, in case his schedule depended on the day of the week. At that time, I didn't know exactly when it would happen."

Paul closed his eyes and bit his lip.

"You ran to the Rice home last Wednesday?" Pete asked.

"No. I took Dylan's car. I didn't leave as early as I'd planned, so I had to get there fast. I was relieved that Dylan didn't find out."

Paul Norman's eyes widened as he shot a quick glance at Caitlin.

"Did you plan to strike Nicholas Rice with Dylan's car?" Pete asked.

"No. I couldn't ask to use Dylan's car, and I couldn't chance him catching me if I tried to borrow it again. He'd have made me tell him why I wanted to use it. He always knows when I am lying. I'd never have gotten away with it."

"Where did you get the car you used?" Pete asked.

"I heard Logan talking about this guy he works with who always needs money. I asked that guy if I could borrow his car. I said I'd pay two hundred dollars. I didn't want to risk his saying, 'No way.' He told me to come back last Monday, with the money, and he'd give me the keys. When he gave me the keys, he told me where his car would be parked. He said I had to use it the next morning, and I had to have it back by seven. I hadn't yet decided when I would do it. I was glad to have the day decided for me. I knew the times wouldn't be a problem. Mr. Rice always ran past that corner between a quarter to six and six fifteen."

Paul cringed.

"I thought you said he didn't always run the same route," Martin said.

"After I'd tracked his pattern for a while, he started changing parts of it. For whatever reason, that part stayed the same."

"How often did Dylan help you track Rice?" Martin asked.

"Never. I'd never have been able to get him out of bed that early. If I'd succeeded, he'd have been half-asleep. He'd have been no help at all."

"Lots of guys go the extra mile for their sisters, especially younger sisters. Are you telling me Dylan wouldn't even give up an hour of sleep for you?" Pete asked.

"Dylan would do anything for me. He gave up a whole night's sleep when he caught me with a bottle of Mom's sleeping pills. Somehow, he knew I planned on taking them all."

Paul Norman gasped. He reached for his daughter's hand, and squeezed it.

"Sorry, Dad. I couldn't take it anymore. Dylan stayed up all night with me. He held me, and I cried 'til I couldn't cry anymore. He told me he couldn't deal with me killing myself. He said he'd blame himself for not knowing and stopping me. He made me promise to tell him if I ever felt that desperate again. Dylan's the best. Now he's in jail, and it's all my fault."

Caitlin's face collapsed into her hands. She sobbed uncontrollably.

Tears ran down her dad's cheeks.

Pete waited a minute, then said, "Dylan seems very protective. Too protective to let you carry out the mission against Nicholas Rice without his help."

"He wouldn't have helped me with this any more than he'd watch me overdose on sleeping pills. He'd have made sure I couldn't do it. That's why I couldn't tell him about my plan. Even more important, I didn't want to get him involved. I was willing to get myself in trouble, but not Dylan." Tears flowed unchecked down Caitlin's cheeks and dripped on her shirt.

"What did you wear when you went out to watch Nicholas Rice?" Martin asked.

"Dylan's down parka and a ski mask."

"Why did you wear Dylan's jacket and not your own?" Martin asked.

"Because navy is harder to see when it's dark outside," Caitlin said, breaking eye contact.

"It was pretty warm for a ski mask some of those mornings, wasn't it? Wasn't Nicholas Rice either suspicious or alarmed to see someone wearing a ski mask when it was that warm?" Martin asked.

"He might have been if he'd seen me wearing it. I pulled it off as soon as I saw him, before he noticed me."

"What kind of vehicle did Logan's friend loan you?" Martin asked.

"A Buick LeSabre."

"You looked it over that carefully?" Martin asked.

"No, I had to know what it was, so I could find it when I went to pick it up."

"Do you remember the color?" Martin asked.

"Yes, black."

"You must have had help determining Nicholas Rice's schedule and path," Martin said. "One person could never do that alone. Remember, we can only help you if you tell the truth. Even if he wasn't otherwise involved, Dylan helped you with that part, didn't he?"

"No. It's not like I went one morning and discovered everything. I spent week after week determining Mr. Rice's schedule."

"What did the guy who loaned you the Buick think you were going to do with it?" Martin asked.

"I don't think he cared. He never asked. I think he was happy to have the money."

"Tell me the name of the person you borrowed the car from," Pete said.

"Kevin Douglas."

"When did you last speak with Kevin Douglas?" Pete asked.

"When he gave me the keys. I didn't tell him what happened, but he must know. He has the number for my cell, but he hasn't called."

"What did you do with the keys to the LeSabre?" Pete asked.

"As I ran away, I threw them in one of the pine trees on the median. I was scared to death I'd be caught with them."

"Tell me what happened after you picked up the car on Tuesday," Martin said.

"I waited for Mr. Rice to reach the intersection where it happened. I just wanted to bump him and send him sprawling. I figured, worst case, he'd end up in the emergency room. They'd patch him up and send him home," Caitlin said between sobs.

Paul Norman looked miserable.

"If that was the plan, how did Nicholas Rice end up pinned against a tree?" Pete asked.

"Mr. Rice ran along the median strip on Wheelock," Caitlin wept. "When he was almost to the street in front of me, between two sections of the median, I tried to start the car. It wouldn't start. By the time I got it going, he was almost all the way across the street. I floored the gas pedal. I wanted to reach him before he was back on the median. It didn't work. He either saw or heard me and took off. I was about to blow the only chance I had to make things better at home. I went up over the curb after him. I planned to slam on the brakes and slow down before I struck him. I was going too fast. The front tires exploded. I couldn't steer away from Mr. Rice." Caitlin's face sought refuge in the shelter of her tightly cupped hands.

After several seconds, she continued, "I'll never forget the look on his face as he collapsed on the hood. He was pinned between the bumper and the tree. I was sure I'd killed him. I wish I'd known he wasn't dead. I should have checked. I could have told him how sorry

I was. I could have called 911. Please believe me, I wouldn't have left him alone. I'd have stayed until the ambulance arrived, even though they'd have arrested me."

Caitlin was crying so hard, both Pete and Martin strained to understand the last few statements.

A tear ran down Paul's cheek.

"I can't sleep. If I take Benadryl to fall asleep, I dream about the look on Mr. Rice's face. I know I deserve whatever I get and more. Please, let Dylan go. He didn't do anything. It was me. It was only me. I never told anyone. I didn't want anyone to stop me. I should have told you this last night. Then Dylan wouldn't have been arrested for my stupidity. I can't do this anymore. I wish I could trade my life for Mr. Rice's."

"Nicholas Rice is still alive, Caitlin," Pete said.

"Is he going to live?"

"The note Martin handed me when he returned was about Nicholas Rice. He regained consciousness. Time will tell, but that's a good sign."

Caitlin looked amazed. "Can I go see him? I want to tell him and his family how sorry I am."

"You might be able to work that out. Let's see what happens," Pete said.

"I have to talk to Dylan. I need to tell him I didn't mean to hurt him. I have to tell him how sorry I am."

"In due time," Pete said.

Paul Norman embraced his daughter. "I'm sorry, Caitlin. I'm so sorry I did this to you."

After Caitlin signed her confession, Pete and Martin escorted her to Martin's car. They didn't turn Caitlin over to a uniformed officer. Contrary to normal procedure, the two investigators took her to juvenile detention and had her booked.

Knowing Nicholas Rice regained consciousness might help her cope. Not willing to risk it, they spoke with three people, ensuring she was put on suicide watch.

FIFTY-THREE

Back at headquarters, Martin turned the conversation to the serious. "The county attorney isn't going to be thrilled with Caitlin's confession."

"Yeah, I know," Pete agreed. "The picture-perfect interview would have had the attorney staying in the interview room. Sometimes we can't provide the picture-perfect. Sometimes we have to settle for what's handed to us. Besides, why should we do all the work?" He smiled and shrugged.

He looked serious as he continued, "Caitlin had a promising life ahead of her. If Nick Rice recovers, she may still be able to make something of it. Even so, she'll never be the same."

"I know. It scares me to think how kids react when they hear their parents argue. Remember what the Bureau of Criminal Apprehension psychologist said—even if a teenager knows right from wrong, teenage brains are less able to perceive consequences or quell impulses. No wonder they can make such crappy decisions. Look at Caitlin's world. Her family is a mess, but she loves her brother. She couldn't let him take the blame for her actions. I think Dylan might have stayed the course, even if it meant going to prison. Appears he's closely attuned to his sister's emotional state. He probably blames himself for not anticipating what she did and stopping her."

"I'll recommend leniency to the county attorney. The video of Caitlin's confession will support the validity of that. And she's a juvenile. That will work in her favor."

"I agree. You know, both kids are going to need counseling," Martin said.

"The whole Norman family needs counseling. And what about the Rice family? How do you think Heather Rice will react if and when she learns the motive behind the attack on her husband?"

"Oh God," Martin moaned. "You know, Pete, I'm as exhausted as Caitlin looked. Do you want to work on reports, or call it a day?"

"We have a few hours of work to prepare the reports the county attorney requires on Monday. Would you rather do it tonight, or tomorrow, Martin?"

They decided to do the reports before they went home. Knowing it meant tomorrow was theirs to spend as they wished was an incentive, and it provided a spark of energy.

Early Saturday morning, as they walked out to the parking lot, Pete said, "I'm happy for the Rice family—that Nick regained consciousness. His family may now be able to begin recovering from that nightmare."

"Yeah, great news. How did you remain so deadpan when I returned to the interview room and handed you that note? I was waiting for you to break into a smile. I wondered how Caitlin and her dad would react if you did."

"I took theater in college to prepare for this career." This time Pete smiled. "Hey, you haven't mentioned your matrix in days. Did it help with this case?"

"Would have," Martin laughed, "if you'd given me an opportunity to keep up. Working only twenty hours per day might do that. The matrix did help me eliminate some of the kids and the waiter. How about if we go through it on Monday? I'll show you."

"It's a date," Pete agreed.

That reminded him about getting together that same evening with Katie Benton.

Pete called Katie late Saturday morning and arranged to pick her up at six. "That way we'll have time for dinner," he said. "Where would you like to go?"

"Surprise me. I like McDonald's, Burger King, and Wendy's."

"Oh, I had my heart set on Subway."

"Fortunately for you, you're making the reservation," she chuckled.

He arrived a few minutes early.

Katie was ready and waiting. That was one more thing he liked about her.

They had a leisurely dinner at the St. Paul Hotel.

Pete didn't fall asleep. He was proud of himself.

After dinner, they walked the few blocks to the History Theatre and spent the time before the play talking. Before long, the lights dimmed and the play began.

Pete rested his head on Katie's shoulder. In a matter of minutes, he was breathing deeply—sound asleep.

Katie smiled. She was pleased he'd kept their date.

Acknowledgments

My thanks to Don Gorrie, retired chief investigator, Ramsey County Medical Examiner's Office, for his sage advice and for recruiting some of his law enforcement friends to assist in this endeavor; to Bill Martinez, senior commander, Homicide and Robbery Unit, St. Paul Police Department, for helping me get the facts straight regarding his unit; to Keith Mortenson, retired commander, St. Paul Police Department, for spoon-feeding me the facts and not relying on caller ID to screen my calls after I became a pest; to Tom Motherway for lending his expertise and doing a reality check on the "final" draft; to Steve Zaccord, fire marshal, St. Paul Fire and Rescue, for schooling me on his department's response protocols; to Dr. Marc Conterato, Minneapolis emergency medicine physician, for assisting with the medical aspects—thrice. Errors in any of these areas are the result of my misinterpretation or misapplication of the information these people so generously shared.

To Perla Cendejas and Jayne at Johnson Senior High for informing Pete and Martin about school schedules and protocols in today's high schools.

I also thank Deb Harper, Pam McCord, Rick Winter, Tara Kennedy, Gale Hawkinson, Brittany McCord, and Marly Cornell for their proofreading and editorial expertise; Christopher Smith for being quick to share his computer and photographic expertise; and Dale Smith for answering my questions about cars and helping with several areas of research.